the GIRLS of SKYLARK LANE

ALSO BY ROBIN BENWAY

Emmy & Oliver

Far from the Tree

A Year to the Day

the GIRLS of SKYLARK LANE

ROBIN BENWAY

HARPER
An Imprint of HarperCollins*Publishers*

The Girls of Skylark Lane

For information, address HarperCollins Children's Books, a division of HarperCollins Publishers, 195 Broadway, New York, NY 10007.

Library of Congress Control Number: 2023948474
ISBN 978-0-06-331159-6

Typography by Julia Feingold
24 25 26 27 28 LBC 5 4 3 2 1

First Edition

For my mom

The best softball player I know

CHAPTER 1

AGGIE

"Dad. Dad. Dad." Twelve-year-old Aggie leaned forward as much as her seat belt would allow her, just in case her dad hadn't been able to hear her from five feet away. *"Daaaad."*

"Aggie." Her dad's voice had that tone of mild exasperation that comes from driving eight hours down the California freeways, with only Starbucks and gas-station bathroom breaks to shake up the flat monotony. "I'm right here. You can just ask me."

Next to Aggie, her twin sister, Jac, was either ignoring the conversation or couldn't hear it at all due to the noise-canceling headphones covering her ears. She was watching a YouTube video like it was about to reveal the meaning of life, her eyes wide and riveted. Like and subscribe, Aggie thought to herself, then turned back toward her dads.

"I think Jack the Rat is hungry," she said, wrapping her arms around the front passenger seat and stretching out her back.

Her dad turned around in the passenger seat, his sunglasses falling down his nose a bit so he could see her. "How on earth can you tell?"

Aggie glanced back toward the trunk of their SUV, where their beloved pet Jack the Rat and his cage, food pellets, water bottle, and exercise wheel had been banished. Both Aggie and Jac had argued for him to share the back seat with them, but both of their dads put their collective foot down at that.

Aggie loved her dad and papa but they sometimes really lacked a sense of adventure.

"I can tell because he looks feisty," she said, and indeed, Jack's whiskers seemed to be quivering a little more than usual.

"He's a rat," her dad said. "He always looks feisty. That's literally his only job in life, to look feisty."

Jac looked up and pulled her headphones off one ear. "Like and subscribe!" Aggie could hear a bubbly girl's voice saying, and she smirked to herself. "What's wrong?" Jac asked.

"I think Jack the Rat is *starving*," Aggie told her.

Their dad sighed from his spot behind the steering

wheel. "If there's one thing Jack the Rat is not, it's starving. He's fine. He has organic food and filtered water. He's moving from one major metropolitan city to another in a luxury vehicle—"

Aggie's dad snorted a little, and Aggie could tell that she—and Jack—were going to lose this battle.

"—and considering that his ancestors probably scrounged for food in garbage cans and on subway tracks, I would say that Jack the Rat can cool his tiny paws for an hour or so until we get to our new house."

Jac peeked over the back seat at his cage. "He looks feisty."

"See?" Aggie said, feeling the flush of victory that only comes from when a sibling agrees with you. "I *told* you."

Regardless of whether or not he was hungry, Jack the Rat did indeed live a very plush life. The sisters had begged their dad and papa for at least a year for a pet—a cat, a puppy, a rabbit—anything that they could care for and snuggle at night and pet its furry ears. And of course, because once again their dads had *zee*-ro sense of fun and excitement, they said no.

Unfortunately, this conversation coincided with the girls' Pixar movie phase, and they were nearly catatonic with joy after watching *Finding Nemo*. They begged for an aquarium full of exotic sea creatures, and their parents finally negotiated them down to one—"One and that is *it*"—goldfish. Aggie and Jac were thrilled and had even settled on a name for their soon-to-be-beloved pet: Sushi.

And then they watched *Ratatouille*.

Game over.

At first, Jac hadn't been exactly delighted to share a name with their new rescue rat, but that was the name that his previous owner had given him and Aggie pointed out that he had already been through enough trauma and changing his name would probably be the final thing that did him in. "Here's hoping," her dad had muttered under his breath, which earned him dirty looks from both girls.

But true to his species, Jack the Rat was a survivor, and Aggie reached back now and pressed her fingertip into the cage, which he sniffed excitedly until he realized that it was just Aggie and not a delicious food pellet. "I think Jack's nervous about moving," she said.

She watched as her dad and papa exchanged a quick glance in the front seat. They did that sometimes when they thought Aggie and/or Jac couldn't see them. It was sort of cute how they thought they were being subtle about it. "I'm serious," Aggie said. "He's just an animal. He doesn't understand."

Jac replaced her headphones, no longer worried about Jack the Rat's welfare, but then held out a bag of jelly beans to Aggie, who gratefully accepted it and began fishing through it for the orange and yellow ones. Sometimes being a twin was annoying, but sometimes it worked out really well in her favor. Jac only liked the pink and green jellies, which made them one of the few things they had been able to share recently without devolving into an argument.

It was weird, Aggie thought as she chomped down on a jelly bean, how you could look just like someone and still feel so different from them.

The crisp sugar coating felt sticky sweet on her tongue as she watched the landscape go by. They had already made it through the worst part of the trip from San Francisco to Los Angeles, that long part of the 5 freeway that always seemed to take hours and hours and hours. They had stopped in Buttonwillow for lunch, which was Aggie's favorite town name ever. Jac's favorite was Zzyzx, and they always had fun trying to pronounce it, but Aggie had a soft spot for Buttonwillow. It sounded like something from a cartoon show that she used to watch when she was younger (and to be honest, the kind of show she wishes she was still young enough to watch), a place where animal families would live in little toadstool houses and have escapades that always ended well.

Aggie guessed her dads had a point when they said

that she had a wild imagination. Especially because, in truth, Buttonwillow had mostly gas stations, convenience stores, and lots and lots of open space.

The problem with a long drive to their new home, Aggie had started to realize around Hour Four in the Car, was that it gave her a lot of time to think. And having a lot of time to think meant a lot of time to worry. Every so often, she'd glance over at Jac, who was either snoozing with her mouth open (yes, of course Aggie took a picture), reading a graphic novel, or watching YouTube videos. Aggie tried to do the same, of course, but she kept losing her place or looking out the window for so long that she'd lose track of what was happening on her phone screen, until the worry would build up so big in her brain that there wasn't room for anything else.

Aggie had always been the worrier. Even in baby photos, Jac had a serene smile on her little face, with Aggie right behind her with a suspicious frown. "State your name, state your business!" her papa used to joke whenever they scrolled through old photos on their hard drive, and it was usually funny, but Aggie was the oldest twin by two minutes and she took it seriously.

And if Jac wasn't going to worry about things, well, then Aggie was just going to have to do it for her.

The worries seemed to click through her brain

as fast as the green freeway signs passed overhead: What if they weren't able to make any new friends? What if Jac made new friends and she didn't? What if their new school was too big and she got lost? What if their new house had termites and one day it fell down around them? What if she missed her old home, her old friends, her old city so much that it hurt? What if she missed them more because she could never get them back again?

Aggie shifted in her seat, her legs sticking to the warm leather car seat. Moving at the end of August wasn't exactly ideal, especially under the hot sun in the back seat of a car.

She knew in her brain that she could go to her parents and tell them all of her worries. They were always there for her, she *knew* that, had always been there to listen to her complain about bad teachers in second grade, mean kids in third, missed soccer goals in fourth. But over the past few months, her worries had shifted into things that couldn't quite be described in words, leaving Aggie feeling slightly adrift, like her dads had strapped her into a life vest, but this time, rather than bringing her home, it had only carried her further away from shore.

"Hey, remember how people used to roast ants using the sun and a magnifying glass?" Jac complained grumpily, pulling one headphone off of her ear.

Their papa reached forward to turn up the AC and said nothing, which was probably for the best. Responding to Jac when she was cranky had the same effect as poking a bear with a stick: Not Great.

Jac grumbled as she turned back to her phone, straightening her sunglasses a little.

Aggie knew she could talk to her twin, too, could go into Jac's room and flop down on her bed and stay there even after Jac complained that she was messing up her freshly washed sheets. But the problem was that she had never *had* to explain anything to Jac before. Jac had always just *known*, had been able to sense that something was wrong with Aggie. Aggie may have been two minutes older, but Jac had started speaking first, and in fact had spoken so well that Aggie saw no need to pipe up at all. "The spokesperson," their dads called Jac with equal parts affection and exasperation, and anyway, eventually Aggie did start speaking, so it all worked out.

But even if Aggie could talk just fine now, sometimes she wasn't sure what exactly to *say*.

"We're almost there!" their papa said, pointing toward the Los Angeles skyline. There were a bunch of buildings that Aggie didn't recognize, not the way she recognized the ones in San Francisco, and she felt her stomach burn in a way that she couldn't decide was good or bad.

"The light doesn't look like this anywhere else in the world," their dad said, pointing toward the honeyed sunset sky, the clouds tinged with hints of pink and lavender, just like Aggie's old bedroom.

She wondered what her new room would look like, smell like, if it would feel like staying in a hotel, rather than a home. And the closer they got to their new neighborhood, chugging their way down the 101 freeway through a maze of cars and gas stations and palm trees, Aggie felt both her nerves and excitement increase, tangling up together in her stomach until she couldn't sort them out, couldn't imagine one without the other.

"Hey," Jac said suddenly, and Aggie turned her head to see Jac holding out the last of the jelly beans, only the orange and yellow ones left behind.

"Thanks," Aggie replied, taking it from her twin, her mirror, her person. Jac just lowered her sunglasses a bit so she could wiggle her eyebrows at Aggie.

It would have been a really sweet, lovely moment between them, two sisters navigating a new adventure together.

If only Jack the Rat, who was in fact starving and had gotten a whiff of the jelly beans, hadn't chosen that exact moment to escape his cage.

CHAPTER 2

JAC

Jac had spent a lot of time imagining what the moment would be like when they pulled into their new neighborhood.

Like, a *lot*.

It had taken her a week to decide on her outfit. Something that wouldn't wrinkle (because her dads insisted on *driving* rather than flying like normal people), something that wasn't too flashy but would also stand out. Something that would tell people who she was, but not too much. Jac enjoyed the thrill of mystery, the hope against hope that someone might look at her and think, *Who's that?* even if she was just an almost thirteen-year-old with two dads and a sister who looked just like her.

And Jac truly loved Aggie with all of her heart, would always feel that twin bond with her sister, would hurt if Aggie was injured, but honestly? Having another person in the world who looked just like you was a real good way to not be original.

Anyway. Back to her outfit.

She had finally chosen her dad's old NASA T-shirt, a shirt that she had pulled out of the rag bag and immediately hacked off the sleeves and neck, then tied it up around her waist. "Hey!" he had said when he saw her wearing it. "Why does that look cuter on you than it did on me?"

"Finders keepers," Jac had said airily (again, *mystery*) but she had been quietly thrilled about his compliment for the rest of the day.

So the shirt was sorted. Next were the jeans, which again, she had taken the scissors to. They had been some boring old pair back when she was in sixth grade, but now that she was almost in seventh, they had frayed hems and ripped knees. "What are you doing?" Aggie had screeched when she saw Jac gleefully hacking into the denim. Aggie liked everything prim and proper and pressed. She even ironed her jeans, which Jac wouldn't have believed if she hadn't seen it with her own eyes.

"MYOB," Jac had replied without looking up, afraid that if she looked away, she'd stop hacking into the jeans and hack into her own finger.

"Do Dads know you're doing this?" Aggie demanded.

"Nope," Jac said, her tongue caught between her teeth as she worked. "They'll probably send me to juvenile hall. Oh well, it will have been worth it."

She grinned to herself as Aggie huffed and flounced away. There was no thrill quite like ruffling your sister's feathers.

But back to her outfit.

The shoes were easy, of course. Her red high-top Converse sneakers, the ones she had gotten last year for her twelfth birthday and had immediately taken outside and started dragging around in the street.

"They can't look *new*," she had explained to her parents when they started exclaiming about how they were brand-new and what was she doing, but honestly? The fact that she even had to explain that to them just showed how *old* they were. What kind of almost teenager would show up at school in brand-new-looking shoes? Well, Aggie, probably. But definitely not Jac, that's for sure.

Anyhoodle. Outfit.

As they pulled into their new strange city, the one that meant "City of Angels" and kind of looked like heaven from a distance, Jac strategically applied her scented lip balm. She had already gone through two tubes of it so far, not from use but from carelessness. One had gotten lost somewhere in the depths of her backpack; another had accidentally ended up in the dryer, along with the rest of her family's laundry. (And wow, had that been a bad cherry-flavored day. You would have thought Jac had burned the house done with how upset everyone was. Like none of *them* had ever made a mistake before? Jac felt insulted.)

She was guarding this third tube with her life, or more accurately, guarding it in the pocket of her newly styled old jeans. And as they made their way up through a winding street full of shopping centers and fancy coffee places and laundromats, she felt a tiny burst of excitement. This was her chance to be someone new, someone different, an individual. "Who's that cool girl?" she imagined people saying as she casually climbed out of their car, her hair blowing in the breeze just so. Jac had even secretly practiced her smile in the bathroom mirror back in their old house in San Francisco, just enough to look friendly but not overeager.

There was just one problem: Aggie looked like she was going to barf.

"Hey," Jac said, then held out her coveted package of jelly beans.

And that's when things took a turn.

Jack the Rat came flying out of the cage just as

their car turned into their neighborhood. "Oh no! Jack!" Aggie screamed.

"Which Jack?" their dad cried just as Jack leapt from the back seat onto the center console, clearly thrilled at his newfound freedom and vowing to not waste a second of it. Their dad turned so fast that his glasses flew off his head, which was unfortunate because he happened to be driving the car at the time.

He then yelled things that neither Jac nor Aggie were allowed to repeat. Their papa, on the other hand, immediately snatched his drink out of the console so Jack the Rat couldn't get to it.

"Jack!" Jac screamed. She saw his pink tail starting to disappear toward the steering wheel and tried to grab for it, but all that did was (a) make Aggie scream again and (b) make her dad swerve the car as Jack scrambled over his lap and detoured onto the armrest.

"THE WINDOW" Aggie cried.

"Good riddance," their dad said under his breath.

Jac reversed course, and instead of trying to grab Jack, she instead reached around the driver's side and quickly pressed the child window lock button so that Jack wouldn't accidentally lower the window and fling himself out of it, the way Aggie had almost done when she was five and obsessed with the idea of skydiving.

"WILL SOMEONE GET THIS RODENT OFF OF

ME?" their dad yelled as he swerved the car back just in time to avoid hitting a mail truck. The mailwoman looked at them with a less-than-thrilled expression as they zoomed past her.

"We are *never* getting our mail on time after this," their papa moaned.

"He's going across the dashboard!" Aggie cried, which Jac thought was a little bit unnecessary, since they could all see Jack scrambling across it. Aggie unfastened her seat belt and tried to reach past the front seats for him.

"We are in a moving vehicle. Why is your seat belt off?" her dad demanded, but then braked for a squirrel that had the unfortunate timing of trying to run across the road right then.

Also unfortunately, Jack saw the squirrel, too.

"Oh no!" Jac yelled as Jack doubled back across the dashboard, leapt down onto the navigation screen, past the gear shift, and toward the girls. Jac made a grab for him, but he was too fast, squirming past her and going down by Aggie's feet.

"It's like trying to catch an eel!" Aggie said, grabbing at him.

"When have you ever tried to catch an eel?" Jac asked, breathless from the excitement.

"I'm just saying!"

"Can we pull the car over, please?" their papa said.

Jack the Rat must have heard them because he hurried into the front seat, probably aware that stopping the car would mean going back into his cage, and he was having way too much fun. These humans! The sounds they could make when they were upset! He hadn't had this much attention in *weeks*, and it was glorious. He let out a few squeaks of delight, which only seemed to make everyone even more excited.

"Jack, get back here!" Jac cried, pointing to his cage.

Aggie just looked at her. "Oh, yeah, that'll work."

Jac had been just about to say something, but then their dad turned on to Skylark Lane and screeched to a halt in front of what Aggie and Jac would later realize was their new house. At the moment, though, all they could focus on was Jack bouncing off the windshield and then ricocheting off of it like a fly ball, sailing over the front seats, going over Aggie's and Jac's heads.

"Oh no!" Aggie screamed.

"Jack!" Jac cried.

They both grabbed for him.

And that was why, instead of looking cool and mysterious upon arriving in their brand-new neighborhood, Jac emerged red-faced and panting from the car, holding up Jack the Rat while screaming, "I *got* you, you little weasel!"

It was definitely not the entrance she had been planning on making.

There was only one person outside, not the crowd of curious onlookers that Jac had been imagining in the days leading up to their move, and she supposed she should be grateful for that. A man was watering his lawn across the street, his mouth open as he watched the four of them (well, five if you counted Jack the Rat, but Jac wasn't too sure that her dads considered him a member of the family at this point in time) tumble out of the car.

"Get them a pet, you said," their dad was muttering, brushing invisible rat dirt off his jeans. "Teach them responsibility, you said."

"Well, she caught it," their papa replied. "I don't know how much more responsible you can get."

"It's a him, not an it!" Aggie cried, leaping out of the car and running over to Jac's side. "Is he okay? Is he bleeding?"

Jack just squeaked again and gave her cheek a wet-nosed kiss. He couldn't wait for his next car ride. He wondered if he could somehow get up on the roof next time. Wouldn't that be exciting!

"He's fine," Jac said, wiping her hair off her damp forehead and out of her eyes. She wasn't sure if she was flushed with the exertion of catching Jack or of the embarrassment of her own hubris. Why had she spent so much time worrying about her outfit, her shoes, her everything? No one even cared that they had moved in.

"Hi!" her papa called to the man with the hose, who was still—understandably—staring at them. "We're the new neighbors!"

The man waved in response, looking like he might go call his real estate agent immediately and put a "for sale" sign on his house.

"Well, he hates us," their dad muttered under his breath.

Aggie was still fawning over Jack the Rat, so she didn't see the girl ride up on her bike. She looked short, even while sitting down, even shorter than Jac, who was very annoyed at the 1.2 inches that Aggie held over her. Her brown hair looked tangled in that bike-riding way, and she had grubby sneakers on her feet that Jac couldn't tell were intentionally dirty or not.

"Nice catch," she said, nodding toward Jac and Jack.

"Thanks," Jac said, mostly because her parents had taught her to say thank you whenever someone paid her a compliment, even when it was a compliment about being able to catch a rodent in midair with one hand.

"See ya," the girl said, then casually rode off down the street.

Aggie and Jac watched her ride off as their dads went in search of the one house key that they both thought the other had.

"Did we just make a friend?" Aggie asked.

"Ha," Jac scoffed, then let Jack settle on her shoulder, the way he always liked to do on lazy weekend mornings. He curled into her contentedly, like he hadn't wreaked havoc for the past five minutes. "I doubt it."

But secretly, secretly, secretly . . .

She hoped they had.

CHAPTER 3

AGGIE

The night before the first day of school, Aggie couldn't sleep.

This was nothing new for her, but at least in years past, she had had the familiarity of her bedroom, her house, the view out of the kitchen window that just barely—if you dragged out a step stool, stood on your tippy-toes, and leaned *reaaallllly* far to the left—had a view of the Golden Gate Bridge. But now, lying in the dark in a brand-new bedroom that still smelled faintly of fresh paint, everything just felt a little too . . . strange.

The past week had been a blur of new things, a little bit too much for Aggie's liking. Her parents had been so busy settling in, her papa moving furniture around several times before it was to his liking, her dad doing boring grown-up things like hiring gardeners to mow their lawn and electricians to come fix the wonky light in the living room that kept turning on at three a.m. and scaring everyone half to death. ("But why would a burglar turn *on* the light?" Jac had asked from the stairs, still half-asleep, her bedhead sticking up on one side, and the thought was enough to keep Aggie up for the rest of the night. She had never had to worry about someone breaking into their fifth-floor apartment back in San Francisco.)

Aggie had never liked new things. She liked old familiar things, things that she could count on, that were reliable in their consistency. And when you put three hundred new things all together in a new space—like, say, middle school, just as an example—Aggie's anxiety ramped up until it felt like she had electricity in her fingers and toes, all of that nervous energy trying to shoot out of her because her own body could no longer contain it.

Needless to say, it didn't make for a great night of sleep.

She knew she shouldn't look at the clock, but she glanced at it anyway. Their dads didn't let them keep electronics in their rooms after bedtime, so she had an old digital clock whose neon numbers seemed to mock her more and more every time she looked at them. 10:59. 11:24. 12:07.

Aggie turned over and rubbed her face against

Mr. Hopalong, the stuffed rabbit she had had since she was a baby. Jac had packed away all of her stuffed animals when they moved, saying that she was in middle school now and she didn't need them. Aggie had watched her from the doorway and then gone to her own bedroom and reassured Mr. Hopalong that she would never pack him away and that she was clearly twins with a *monster.* She wondered if Jac regretted that now, if she was also lying wide awake in her new bedroom across the hall, gazing up at the ceiling and all the new, unfamiliar shadows on the walls.

Probably not. In fact, Aggie could hear her sister softly snoring even from a room away, and she once again wondered how she could be so different from someone who looked exactly like her.

She had just looked at the clock again—1:13—when she heard footsteps in the hall, followed by a quiet muffled "*Ow,*" and she had immediately relaxed. That was her papa, who was notorious in his clumsiness and was always either tripping over something or stubbing his toe.

"Papa?" she half called, half whispered.

A few seconds later, her already-ajar bedroom door was pushed open. "Aggs?" her papa whispered. "What are you doing up? Do you know what time it is?"

"I've known what time it is for the past two hours,"

she replied, sitting up on her elbows. "Did you break a toe again?"

"Not yet." He sighed and came into her room. "I was just checking on you and Jac, making sure you weren't being smothered in blankets." He nudged her shoulder. "Scoot."

Aggie scooted, moving over so that her dad could stretch out next to her. "Can't sleep?" he asked, and she shook her head. "Is it because of Jac's snoring?"

Aggie giggled at that, and she felt her papa laugh next to her. "Don't tell her I said that or she'll put hair remover in my shampoo bottle," he said, and Aggie curled up against him, grateful for both the familiarity and the darkness that let her hide her face. Sometimes it was easier to talk when nobody could see you.

"I can hear you thinking," her papa said after a few minutes of silence. "Wanna talk?"

Aggie shrugged. "About what?"

"Oh, I don't know, maybe the fact that it's in the middle of the night and you're wide awake, probably worrying about starting a new school tomorrow and whether or not you'll make friends and if your teachers are nice or assign homework on Fridays. I'm just spitballing, though." Even in the dark, Aggie could hear him smile.

"Am I that predictable?" she muttered.

Her papa shrugged. "Not predictable. Reliable. You've worried about everything since you were a baby."

"But what if they do assign homework on Fridays?" Aggie blurted out. "What if everyone's mean? What if I can't get my locker to open and I'm late for class?"

She felt her papa's hand settle on her head like a soft hat that always fit just right, always kept her warm even when her thoughts were icy cold. "Well, we'll still love you," he told her. "So you've got that going for you. And your sister will be right there with you, too."

"I wish I could be more like Jac," Aggie said softly. "She never worries. She probably hasn't lost any sleep at all this week."

"Jac definitely worries," her papa said, his hand still safely on her head. "She just does it internally. You can't keep it in. And it'd be really weird if you two were exactly alike, don't you think?" He shuddered dramatically at the thought. "Honestly, that would freak Dad and I out way too much. Two kids *exactly* alike? It'd be like a horror movie. All we'd need is a cornfield or an old basement that no one ever goes in."

Aggie giggled despite herself. "You're so weird."

"Thank you," he said. "And don't forget, something is only new once. Tomorrow morning is the last time you'll have to go into a new school."

"Except for high school," Aggie pointed out. "And college. And maybe veterinary school."

"Okay, yes, fine, but work with me here, Aggs." He paused for a second. "Veterinary school?"

"I like animals and it makes me sad when they're sick."

Her papa chuckled under his breath and then wrapped an arm around her, squeezing her tight. "My softhearted kiddo," he said quietly. "You're the best."

"What about Jac?"

"My softhearted, competitive kiddo," he amended. "And Jac's the best, too. Dad and I got extremely lucky in the child lottery. We got the two best ones."

"What if everyone hates me?" she whispered.

"Not possible," he replied immediately. "But if they do, then I hope they get a paper cut every single day of their lives."

Aggie laughed out loud at that, and from across the hall, Jac snorted in her sleep, which made her giggle even harder.

CHAPTER 4

JAC

Aggie wasn't entirely correct.

Jac had her own worries about the first day of school. But she suspected they were different than her sister's.

If her locker didn't open, who cares? She'd tell one of the teachers or maybe the school janitor. If a teacher assigned homework on a Friday, well then, it's just another day. And besides, Jac hadn't earned the unofficial title of Best Procrastinator Ever in her family for *nothing*. How boring and awful would Sunday nights be if you weren't scrambling to finish a diorama or long-term project about thirty-five international bodies of water? (Her parents were obviously less than thrilled about this habit and had spent more than a few weekend evenings up at eleven o'clock at night, blearily gluing tiny pine trees into a shoebox or trying to define the word "isthmus".)

No, those things weren't what Jac was worried about. She had bigger concerns.

Namely, the teacher taking attendance.

This was seventh grade, which would mark Jac's (she had to count on her fingers) ninth first day of school, if you included preschool, which she totally did. That meant it was her ninth time hearing the teacher call out her and Aggie's names.

Their *real* names.

In her dads' defense, they had meant well. To hear them tell the story, they were both delirious from lack of sleep on the night Jac and Aggie had been born, joyfully hysterical over their brand-new baby daughters, crying and laughing and calling their family members and taking photos and high-fiving the nurses and then crying and laughing again.

It was also worth pointing out that their dad was a florist, that he supplied beautiful and luxurious floral arrangements to some of the biggest hotels in San Francisco, and now Los Angeles. He even did celebrity weddings sometimes, which was how Aggie and Jac had ended up as last-minute flower girls in one of the biggest celebrity weddings of all time after the original girls had gotten stage fright, but that was a story for another time and had nothing to do with the first day of seventh grade.

Anyhoodle.

All that to say that her dads' euphoria over becoming parents got a little out of hand, and their florist dad looked out the window and saw the beautiful lilac-colored trees and shrubbery that surrounded the hospital, and well. . . .

That was how Aggie and Jac ended up with the names Agapanthus and Jacaranda.

In some ways, Aggie had it worse. "Aga*pan*thus?!" she would sometimes screech whenever she was feeling particularly wronged by something and wanted to add fuel to the fire. "I sound like some dragon in a fantasy book!"

"You really do," Jac would add, which was not a helpful thing to say and never made the situation better.

Jacaranda wasn't as bad, but still. BUT STILL. She felt like a long-named weirdo in a sea of Annas and Lenas and Stellas and Evies. Because yes, Jacaranda was a beautiful purple-flowered tree that bloomed every June, but was also one of the worst names ever for a twelve-year-old girl.

Which was why it was Jac's goal to always cut the teacher off before she could read her full name off the roll sheet.

If she and Aggie were in the same class, they would look out for each other, of course. Despite all the teasing between them, they both shared the same peer-based embarrassment. Jac had definitely screamed out "AGGIE!" more than once before the teacher could get to the "-*pan*thus?" part of her name. And Aggie had done the same, calling out "That's my sister, Jac!" One time she had even added, "You know, like the mouse in Cinderella!" which had definitely not been the *most* helpful thing she could have contributed to the conversation, but Aggie had meant well.

This year, though, they had separate homerooms. The fact that they even had homeroom in the first place was enough to tell Jac that they were in the big leagues now. This was *seventh grade*. This wasn't some Podunk-elementary-school situation. This was the real deal, and Jac was ready.

She could see the trepidation on Aggie's face as they had climbed the middle school stairs that morning, both of them desperately ignoring their dad waving gleefully from the front seat in the drop-off line. Jac had set her face into a look of cool dispassion (she had read that description in a book once and was determined to use it in real life one day), something she had practiced in the mirror that morning before Aggie had burst into her room demanding to know what she was wearing. As identical twins, they both knew the absolute importance of not dressing alike, whether it was a new situation or not.

Jac was glad she had practiced her expression. Aggie, on the other hand, clearly had not. "Cool dispassion" was nowhere on Aggie's face, and as they climbed the stairs, Jac shot her sister a quick, encouraging, *cool* smile. "Relax," she said. "You look like you're going to the gallows." (Jac had also really gotten into the French Revolution in sixth grade, even dressing as Marie Antoinette for Halloween that year.)

"I *am* relaxed," Aggie shot back, sounding the complete opposite of relaxed, which Jac wisely decided not to mention.

"Okay," Jac said. "I'll see you after school, all right?" She was two minutes younger but often she felt like the big sister, the one blazing a trail in front of Aggie so that nothing would leap out and hurt her. And she felt bad even thinking it, she felt awful, truly, but deep down in the dark place just behind her heart, the place where she kept her worst thoughts, she hoped that she and Aggie didn't have any classes together.

Aggie just nodded, looking like she was going to throw up, and Jac beat a hasty retreat in case that's what was about to happen. (A) she was not great with vomit, and (B) she loved her sister, but she was NOT going to potentially be associated with the girl who barfed on the first day of school.

She set out for her homeroom and took a tiny bit of comfort in knowing that Aggie was doing the same. At least, she *assumed* that her sister wasn't wandering around in a lost haze since she had practically memorized the school map the night before.

Of course, now that she was making her way toward her homeroom class, Jac regretted—just a teeny tiny little bit—not being as planner-oriented as her sister. Everyone just kind of seemed *bigger* than they had in their old school. Jac wasn't exactly short, but all the other kids seemed taller than her, and she found herself sort of craning her neck, looking around for room 302. Then the bell rang and she almost had a heart attack. Surely they could update the system to be less archaic than a shrill bell ringing every hour! It was the twenty-first century! What was next, an armed mob leading them all from class to class? (Jac had *really* liked studying the French Revolution.)

But then she found the 300 building and then room 302, and everyone in the classroom seemed like another average student and not the towering giants that they had been in the hallway. She was also relieved to see that the school was as diverse as her old one in San Francisco had been, with all different kinds of nationalities and kids. She wondered if anyone else had two dads like she and Aggie did.

The room had a big window that let in just enough sunlight to highlight all the leftover summer dust in the room, and the walls had a bunch of those old "READ" posters from the library that her dad and papa would have called "vintage," not old, but Jac knew that that they basically meant the same thing.

It was a fresh start. And if there was one thing Jac loved, it was a fresh start.

CHAPTER 5

AGGIE

Aggie did not love a fresh start.

Aggie liked plans and schedules and routines. She liked spreadsheets, algorithms, straight lines, and color-coordinated shelving systems. She had spent the past three years trying to convince her dads to let her celebrate her birthday at the Container Store. (Aggie was fairly certain she was pretty close to wearing them down.)

She sat very still in her homeroom seat that morning, pretending to be deeply curious about her new notebook. (And really, was there anything better than a new journal or notebook? Aggie almost hated to write in them and ruin their perfect pristineness.) Her ears were warm and her hands were ice cold, so she took turns rotating them in and out of her hoodie pocket. Her bouncing knee, on the other hand, she could do nothing to stop.

Aggie liked who she was. She didn't want to change. She even liked her name, despite her and Jac's protests to their dads about why they couldn't have been an Olivia or Ava or Ruby instead. But sometimes, and only sometimes, she wished she could be more like Jac, her insides more like a still river than a turbulent ocean. Nothing ever fazed Jac, while it felt like everything fazed Aggie.

"Psst!"

Aggie didn't look up at first, since she didn't know anybody and nobody knew her, so why would they be trying to get her attention. Besides, she was very busy staring at the page while doodling an important flower in the margins.

"Hey! Psst! New kid!"

Aggie said a quick, silent prayer that they were talking to some other new kid.

"Hey! New person wearing the purple hoodie!"

Well, crap.

Aggie glanced up to see a girl with short hair, mild buck teeth, and gangly limbs looking back at her. Her expression was a mixture of curiosity, friendliness, and the kind of eagerness that Jack the Rat produced whenever he smelled cheese nearby.

"Me?" she asked.

"Of course you. You're the new kid. You live on my street. I saw you move in."

Aggie started to answer, then realized that this girl hadn't actually asked a question yet. And it didn't seem to matter because she also hadn't stopped talking.

"We haven't had anyone new on our street for *ages*, so everyone knows about you."

Aggie blinked. She wasn't sure if that was a good thing or a bad thing.

"Anyway, we needed some fresh blood. All the other kids on our street are either babies or boring teenagers who can drive." The girl smiled again.

Up at the podium, the teacher paused from taking roll call, then cleared her throat.

Aggie knew all too well what was about to happen next.

"Aga-Aga*pan*—?"

She whipped her head toward the front of the classroom so fast that it felt like it took her eyeballs an extra second to catch up. "HERE!" Her voice was high and shrill, and several of the other kids giggled, which made her face feel like she had a fever. "Here," she said again, hoping she sounded less panicked. "It's Aggie."

"Aggie," the teacher said without looking up,

making a note in her book. "Got it."

When she turned back around, the girl was still staring at her. "You seem like you have fast reflexes," she said, leaning in a little. "Do you ever play—"

The teacher cleared her throat again, but this time it was the other girl whose attention was immediately jerked toward the front of the room. "It's Tink!" she cried. "Just Tink!" Her voice wasn't as shrill as Aggie's had been, and really, it probably wasn't humanly possible for anyone's voice to be like Aggie's, but even so, Aggie recognized that mild panic of an entire room of people about to find out your real, embarrassing name.

When the girl turned back around, Aggie smiled.

An hour later, Aggie knew a lot about Tink.

She had a seven-year-old sister named Josephine and an older brother named Finn. Her mom worked in downtown LA, and they lived with her grandma Isabel just around the corner from Aggie and Jac's house. Tink's grandmother had been there for almost fifty years and said they'd have to carry her out feet first, which is why everything in the house was so old and smelled like powder.

Tink didn't mention her dad, so Aggie didn't ask.

"I also like cats," Tink said as she and Aggie left homeroom together. Or, more accurately, Tink followed Aggie out of homeroom. "Even the feral ones. I used to feed one all the time until Isabel found out." Aggie wondered if she could get away with calling her own grandmother by her first name, then immediately realized that was out of the question. Their grandma Lydia was old-school, as Jac often described her. "Anyway, Isabel has a parrot that never shuts up, so we can't get a cat because it would make the cat lose its mind. It's already making the rest of us *nuts*. Do you know that parrots can live almost eighty years?"

Tink reminded Aggie of one of those old-fashioned toys where you turned the crank in their back and they just kept going and going and going.

"I did know that," Aggie said.

"Cool. And you have a mouse, right?"

"He's a rat, actually." Aggie was pretty sure that Jack the Rat would be offended by anyone referring to him as a mouse.

"A rat!" Tink sounded like Aggie had just told her they were going to Disneyland. (Which was absolutely on Aggie's bucket list, but that was a story for another time.) "I saw him when he came flying out of the car. That was so cool. Can I come see him? Or her? It?"

"Him," Aggie said. "And sure." She was starting to suspect that Tink was one of those lonely people who would suction on to the first person who spoke to them, and she sighed inwardly. "You're too nice," Jac would always tell her. "You have to cut it off at the knees."

But Aggie *was* too nice, and frankly, she didn't really think that was a character flaw, *okay*, Jac? She'd rather talk to a lonely person than imagine them being lonely, after all.

"You can come over after school anytime," Aggie said, since she was fairly certain that Tink didn't have a lot of pressing after-school invitations. "Jack's really friendly. He might nibble you, but it's like a kiss from him."

Tink looked positively elated at the idea of a rat gnawing on her fingers, and despite her unease, Aggie felt that first connection of potential friendship. Anyone who liked Jack the Rat couldn't be all that bad, even if she talked nonstop.

"That would be so cool to meet a rat up close and in person— Oh!"

Aggie looked up at Tink's surprise, only to see Tink looking down the hall at her sister. "You," Tink started to say, pointing at Jac, then pointing back at Aggie before giggling. "Oh my God, you're a twin!"

Aggie sighed. People always acted like she and Jac each had three heads whenever they realized that they were twins. The number of people alone who would come up to them and their dads in stores, on the street, in line at the post office, and immediately start talking about the twins in their own family was too high to count. Aggie guessed that she and her family had seen nearly a hundred photos of smiling lookalikes, strangers pulling them up on their phone and blabbing about their cousins, uncles, sons, whoever. The worst ones were the people who smiled knowingly and said, "Twins?" like they were all in on some big secret. Jac, naturally, had gotten fed up and started answering, "No, clones," in her most drone-like voice while staring at the person, unblinking. The first time she had done it, their dad had almost snorted coffee out of his nose, but now that was just their standard response.

Jac looked up at Tink's outburst, and Aggie immediately saw her sister's eyes narrow. "Jac!" Aggie called, waving at her before her sister could pretend like she hadn't heard them and disappeared around the corner. "C'mere!"

"You named your pet rat after your sister?"

"It's a long story," Aggie replied, even though it really wasn't. "This is my sister, Jac." She very purposefully did not use the word "twin."

Jac came closer to them, her hand wrapped protectively around the solo backpack strap slung over her shoulder. (When had she stopped using the other strap? Aggie wondered. This was new.) Tink was nearly vibrating, she was so excited, and as Jac stepped up to them, Aggie could sense danger.

Jac, you see, was not one for big acts of excitement or affection.

"Hi!" Tink said. "Oh my God, you really do look so much alike! I'm Tink! You have a rat!"

Jac slid her eyes over to Aggie. It was a look that Aggie had long ago become familiar with. Unfortunately. *Who is this person, and for the love of all that is holy, what are you doing with her?* Jac said without speaking a word.

Aggie cleared her throat. "This is Tink."

"I said that already!" Tink was still smiling in a way that kind of made her resemble a rabbit, even though Aggie wasn't sure whether or not rabbits could actually smile. She would have to google that later. "You live down the street from me! Well, actually, my *grandma* lives down the street from *you* and *we* live with *her*, so yeah. I mean, me and my mom and my brother and my little sister. Her name is Josephine. I mean my sister is named Josephine, not my mom. Anyway, we were going to call her Joey but she hates that nickname so when you meet her *definitely* do *not*—"

Jac was shifting her eyes between Tink and Aggie, her face carefully constructed into blankness, or so it would seem. Aggie, on the other hand, had spent nearly every single day of her life with Jac and she knew that dead-eye stare was a ruse. This was Jac summoning all of her strength to barely tolerate someone. She had used the same look on her third-grade teacher, their old mailman who used to pretend to catch her nose when she was a toddler, and anyone who would go on and on about their specific food allergies.

"—mom works nights, so my grandma watches us during the day, well, she doesn't really watch us, she watches TV, she likes Steve Harvey but I think all grandmas like Steve Harvey."

Tink was really going off the rails. Aggie needed to step in now.

"Wow," she said with a smile big enough to (hopefully) make up for Jac's blank expression. "Grandmas are so weird." She didn't really think that, especially because her and Jac's grandma Lydia was *really* cool. She ran an eBay store and did half marathons and always let Aggie and Jac try on her medals when they visited her.

But their grandma was back in San Francisco, and Aggie had a sudden pang of homesickness, which was strange because she was already home.

Right?

"It was nice meeting you," Jac said, "but I don't want to be late to class, especially on the first day."

"Oh, totally!" Tink replied.

"I told her she could come by and meet Jack the Rat at some point," Aggie added.

Jac slid her eyes over to her sister again, and Aggie pointedly did not look back at her. Instead, she turned back to Tink and said, "You can feed him a treat if you want."

Tink's smile got even wider, which Aggie had not thought was possible. "Awesome!" she said. "I'll probably have to bring Josephine with me, but I'll tell her not to talk at *all*. Once she gets going, she does not *stop*." She laughed and shook her head as if to say, *That kid*.

"You don't say." Jac's voice was flat.

"That sounds great," Aggie hurriedly interrupted. "You and Josephine, not Joey."

"Ha! Exactly!" Tink lightly smacked Aggie on the shoulder before reaching out to Jac, who suddenly had the urge to retie her shoelaces and bent down before Tink could hit her, too. "There are so many cool things I can tell you about, too!"

Aggie braced herself for another monologue, but just then the bell rang, and everyone in the hallway started to scatter. "Oops, I'm always late for math because it's all the way over on the other side of the building and there are those stairs that everyone always slips on—pro tip, by the way, do *not* run down those stairs unless you have a death wish—and I don't know why they have to schedule classes so far apart." She took a deep breath and laughed again. "Okay, time to sprint! See you later, alligator! Or alligators, actually!"

Thankfully, Jac waited until Tink was safely around the corner before turning to Aggie. "What," she said, "was *that*."

"She's a *who*, not a what," Aggie said with an eye roll. "And that's Tink. I think she's our neighbor."

"Wow."

"I know. She's—"

"A lot," they both said at the same time. There was a time when that used to annoy Aggie, the fact that they could finish each other's sentences. It was like they were always using the same brain, having the same thoughts, but now, as it felt like Jac was moving further away from her, Aggie felt a sudden surge of safety in being tethered to her sister.

"You better get going so you're not late," Jac said, gesturing down the hall in the complete opposite direction of where Aggie needed to be. Then she paused and added, "You doing okay?"

"Fine," Aggie said, and it was partly true. Just having Jac ask settled something inside of her, their tether tightening. "I already made a friend."

Jac laughed at that as she started to back away down the hall. "Good luck with that!" she called out as she disappeared around the corner. "You're gonna need a Red Bull to keep up with her!"

Aggie was still smiling even after Jac was gone.

CHAPTER 6

JAC

Jac, on the other hand, had yet to make a friend.

That was fine with her, of course. Unlike Aggie, who was always welcoming every stray thing—dog, cat, rat, human, it didn't matter—Jac was more cautious. "Discerning," her dad and papa would often say about her, and it was true and Jac was just fine with that. She understood the value in pulling up the drawbridge and forcing people to swim the moat to get to her.

She glided through her first day, sliding in and out of desks and lunch tables, hoping that she seemed cool and mysterious, the new girl. By the time she made it to her last class of the day, PE, she dressed in the hideous uniform and found herself outside on a softball field.

"Who thought green and yellow were good school colors?" she muttered to herself as she stepped outside. The elastic waistband of the shorts was biting into her waist, and she tugged them down a bit just as she rounded the corner and bumped into Aggie and her new friend, the human who seemed more like a golden retriever.

Tink. That was her name. Jac had questions.

"Hey!" Aggie said. She was wearing the same ugly uniform but Tink had on gray sweatpants, and Jac made a mental note to immediately ask how that was allowed and how she could start doing the same thing.

"Hi!" Tink added brightly, and Jac felt some of her cool, mysterious New Girl vibes slip away.

"Hi," Jac said.

"Whoever chose these colors for a PE uniform needs to see a therapist," Aggie muttered, pulling at the front of her shirt. "Is this even a breathable fabric?"

"I highly recommend telling them that you have an allergy to polyester," Tink said, nodding sagely like she was delivering the secret to life. "We all figured that out last year." And sure enough, as Jac looked around, the majority of kids were wearing gray shirts and sweatpants.

Well then, that settled that. Jac was not a follower,

but she was also not going to wear this uniform if she didn't have to.

"OKAY, LADIES!" their gym teacher, Mrs. Mitchell, yelled. She was wearing a visor that looked like it hadn't left her forehead for the past ten years, and there was a whistle around her neck. "We're going to just jump right in and get warmed up with softball today—"

"Yesss," Tink hissed under her breath.

"—and we're playing against the boys."

Jac rolled her eyes a little and felt a small bond of solidarity when Aggie did the same. "Their idea of gender is seriously from the Stone Age," Jac said.

"Seriously," Tink repeated, and there was a glint in her eye that hadn't been there before. "It's so boomer. I know this one—"

She was cut off by the shrill blow of a whistle, and all three girls jumped. "LET'S MOVE, LADIES!" Mrs. Mitchell cried. "Let's show those boys who's boss!"

"This feels very problematic," Aggie said.

"I already *know* I'm the boss," Jac muttered under her breath.

Tink, however, was already racing forward like she was going into battle. "LET'S CRUSH THEM!" she cried.

Aggie and Jac glanced at each other. "Sigh," Jac

said aloud. "So. Did you know we're both allergic to polyester?"

"I learned that about thirty seconds ago," Aggie replied, and Jac grinned.

At first, the game seemed silly. The late-summer morning fog had burned off, leaving the softball field in a yellow glow of afternoon haze. Aggie and Jac sat next to each other on the bench, gradually moving toward their chance at bat, and Tink stalked back and forth in the dugout, clapping and encouraging each kid as they got up to bat.

"YOU GOT THIS, GONZALES!"

"C'MOOON, MCMURRAY! LET'S GOOOO!"

"EYE ON THE BALL, I FORGOT YOUR NAME!"

"She could power a small city," Jac said, watching Tink clap enthusiastically as the first baseman fumbled the ball and Forgot-Your-Name made it to first base.

"Easily," Aggie agreed, wiping her hands on her knees.

"OKAY, PALMER, IT'S YOUR TURN!" Tink was waving toward the twins.

"Which one?" Jac said, but she knew she was being difficult and that it was Aggie's turn.

Aggie stood up and grabbed one of the bats, giving it a few practice swings as she walked up to home plate. Unfortunately, the momentum made her lose her balance and she stumbled a little, almost face-planting right onto the base.

And a few boys in the outfield started to snicker.

"C'mon, move it in!" the shortstop yelled, and Jac resisted the urge to go up to him and grind his face into the dirt. "Easy out, easy out!"

"YOU GOT THIS, AGGIE!" Tink cheered, but she looked angry, too.

Jac, however, just sat back and got ready to watch the show.

Because here was the thing about Aggie: She had a very big temper. She also had a very long fuse, so it didn't appear too often, but when it did, it was like watching a cyclone suddenly appear over a town, and Jac was the only one on that field who had experience in taking cover.

And judging by the frown lines on her forehead and the brewing anger in her eyes, Jac could tell that the boys laughing and jogging into the infield had rapidly burned Aggie's fuse down to nothing.

Just like a stick of dynamite.

Jac tapped Tink on the shoulder. "Watch this," she said, then gestured toward the field.

Aggie took another practice swing, this time with her feet firmly planted on the ground, and squared her shoulders and bent her knees, just like her dad had taught them when they used to play catch in the park.

The first pitch came fast.

And so did Aggie's swing.

The metal *clang!* of the aluminum bat registered with everyone first, with the ball sailing past all of them seconds afterward, easily clearing the heads of all the kids in the infield and not even descending into the outfield as it made its way toward the field's fence. There was a strange second or two of silence as everyone watched the ball disappear, and Jac sent an admiring smirk toward her sister.

Aggie just flipped the bat to bounce off her fingertips before flipping it back. Their dad had taught them both that trick, and sometimes it came in very handy.

And then Tink lost it.

"PALMERRRRRRR!!!!!! WAY TO GOOOOO!!!!!!" If Tink had been wearing a hat, she would have tossed it into the air, but instead she had to settle for leaping around in a circle, her hands raised in victorious fists as she whooped it up. Any passerby would have thought that Tink was the one who hit the home run, and Jac laughed as she watched Aggie delicately trot around the bases, tapping each one with her toe like she was a ballerina, dragging out her victory for as long as possible.

As soon as she got close enough, Jac high-fived her without saying a word. Sometimes, as both sisters and twins, they didn't have to speak.

Besides, they wouldn't have been able to hear themselves over Tink. Jac wondered if they would need a tranquilizer dart to bring her back down to earth.

After the game, and after the boys' team dragged themselves off the field, Tink came up to the girls. "Listen," she said.

"Do we have a choice?" Jac asked.

"After school. My house. Or actually, my front yard. Be there."

Jac had truly never met anyone like Tink in her life. "Are we . . . doing something?" she asked.

Tink looked around like somebody was listening in on their conversation, then leaned in. "It's a secret."

"Oh my God, Tink, you're at an eight. Bring it down to a four." A girl behind her rolled her eyes behind her glasses, then pushed them up her nose. "Hi. I'm Adriana. Ignore her. She gets too wound up sometimes." Tink kept beaming, though, and Adriana slung an arm around her shoulders. Jac got the distinct feeling that they had been friends for a long time, and she felt a quiet punch of sadness and jealousy in her stomach.

Being cool and mysterious was great and all, but it didn't always lend itself to making friends.

"Can you come over, too?" Tink said, and Adriana looked down at her Apple Watch, tapping it a few times.

"For, like, fifteen minutes," Adriana said without looking up. "I have a fundraising meeting at four thirty. My mom's office might donate to the cause for their monthly charity."

Adriana definitely looked like their age, which is why it was confusing to hear her talk like an adult. When she looked back up, though, she smiled, revealing a mouth of braces covered in colorful rubber bands.

"I run a lemonade stand. Maybe you've heard of it?"

"I . . ." Aggie started to say, then looked over at Jac with a shrug. They had never heard of any specific lemonade stands in their lives. Had anyone? Was that a Los Angeles thing? Jac had been expecting palm trees, sunsets, and maybe a celebrity or two, not lemonade stands.

"Of course they haven't heard of it. Get over yourself," Tink said as Adriana started to dig two business cards out of her backpack and pass them to the twins. "Adri thinks she's famous."

Adriana just rolled her eyes as Jac reached for the card. "I prefer to fly under the radar," she replied. "It's better for business." The card had the words "Handing You Lemons" written in a pretty pink font on it, and "Adriana Gutierrez, Founder and CEO" printed below it, followed by "@handingyoulemons" and all of their social media symbols.

It looked very professional. Jac was fairly certain actual adults with actual businesses had less fancy cards. She was also fairly certain she had never met a CEO her own age before.

"Make sure to follow us on social media!" Adriana said, shoving her glasses back up her nose. "And mention us online for ten percent off your first order!"

"Are you verified yet?" Tink asked, in a note that let them know that she already knew the answer.

Adriana cleared her throat. "I'm working on it." Her smiled dimmed slightly before returning. "Anyway, don't let Tink and her 'go, team, go' thing scare you off. She's really nice, just loud."

"I have a positive attitude and a cheerful disposition," Tink protested, and Adriana squeezed her shoulder.

"Sure," she said, then looked at the twins. "See you later!"

"See you later," Jac replied, glancing at Aggie. It was like looking in a mirror, both of their expressions wary and hopeful at the same time.

What exactly, she wondered, had she and her sister gotten themselves into.

CHAPTER 7

AGGIE

Aggie arrived home two steps before Jac, which meant she was the first one to drop her backpack in the entrance and scream, "HI WE'RE HOME CAN WE GO TO A FRIEND'S HOUSE THEY'RE PROBABLY SAFE."

Their dad came around the corner, wiping his hands on a dish towel. There was a huge stack of rhododendron on the kitchen counter behind him and a smear of dirt on his chambray shirt. "*Probably* safe?" he repeated. "How reassuring."

"We won't actually go in the home," Jac added, dropping her own bag next to Aggie's. Their dad silently pointed at the bags, then up the stairs, and both girls groaned before hauling their bags up to their rooms before thundering back down.

"Please?" Aggie said. "We made a friend—"

"Aggie made a friend," Jac corrected.

"Her name is Tink and she invited us over and she lives with her grandma and you know it's important for us to build friendships for our social developments." Aggie said it all in one breath and then had to pause and catch her breath afterward. "Right?"

Their dad looked somewhere between bemused and concerned. "Where does she live?" he asked, and both girls pointed vaguely past the front door and up the street. "So somewhere in Los Angeles," he said. "Great, I feel much better, thank you."

"She's just around the corner and we won't go in the house," Aggie promised again.

"What about homework? Snack? We haven't even talked about your first day yet."

Parents were so needy, Aggie thought. What did they think happened every day at school? What were they expecting? They never seemed to grasp the fact that a boring day at school was, in fact, a successful one.

"We can talk about it at dinner? And we can do our homework afterward? We have to be done early because Adriana has a meeting with her mom's work about their charity donation."

Now their dad just looked baffled. "The who has a what about huh?"

"Exactly," Jac said. She started to shove Aggie out

the front door, and Aggie let herself be shoved. "We'll be back soon!"

They disappeared so fast that they didn't even hear their dad say "Bye?" in a small, quiet voice.

"I thought you didn't even like her," Aggie said as the two hustled up the street.

"I never said I didn't like her," Jac protested, and Aggie couldn't hold back a loud laugh.

"Yeah, nice try," she said.

"I didn't!" Jac cried.

"No, you just made this face every time she opened her mouth to speak." Aggie turned her mouth down and frowned, then wrinkled her nose.

"I don't ever make that face! You make me look like an old man!"

"You *always* make that face," Aggie said, partly because it was somewhat true and partly because she knew it would annoy her sister to point it out, and who would miss out on an opportunity like that. "Especially when people you don't like start talking."

Jac huffed but didn't argue back, and Aggie felt a small thrill of victory. Winning an argument with her sister would never get old. "Adriana seems cool," Aggie said instead. "Very business-oriented."

"I don't think anyone my own age has ever given me a business card before," Jac said, digging it out of her pocket and examining it again. "These look expensive."

"They're *embossed*," Aggie pointed out. Their dad's business cards for his florist business had the same indentation. He'd be impressed by the details, for sure.

The street was fairly quiet, with most people either at work or already home from school. The soft yellow sunlight dappled through the trees, and Aggie felt tiny bursts of warmth across her skin as they walked toward Tink's house. San Francisco had always felt slightly cold, even on the warmest days, and she kept stepping out into the street so she could feel more of the sun.

"You're going to get hit by a car," Jac said without any real concern in her voice.

Aggie waved her arms around. "What cars? I thought this was Los Angeles. There's supposed to be cars everywhere. The street is empty."

"Maybe nobody wants to drive all the way up into Laurel Canyon," Jac said as Aggie straddled the sidewalk and street, her gait going up and down like a carousel horse. "All the streets are so windy and there's nowhere to park, anyway."

"Is this it?" Aggie said as they walked up to a house that looked . . . well, not like anything they had ever seen before.

Jac glanced down at her phone, then back up at the house. "Of course it is," she sighed. "Of course. It is."

The house was more ramshackle than the others on the street. None of the houses in their neighborhood looked alike, but this one really stood out. It had bright pink bougainvillea flowers and purple winding ivy going up around the front door and toward the second story, and several of the windows were open, letting the sounds of some opera music float down outside. The chimney looked like it was one prayer away from crumbling into smithereens, and the porch was wide, with loose floorboards sticking up here and there.

But it was the front yard that was truly . . . something else.

There were whirligigs everywhere. EVERYWHERE. Rainbow-colored, animal-shaped, reflective and shiny, you name it, it was there. There was just enough of a breeze in the air to send them all fluttering at once, and Aggie had to blink a few times so that her eyes could focus. "This is . . ." She trailed off.

"Wow," Jac said. "Actually, this tracks for Tink."

"It does," Aggie agreed. "What do you think they do when it rains?"

"Get wet."

"HI!" a voice screamed from the distance, and after a few seconds, Tink's head popped out of a second-story window. She had a baseball hat on and was waving frantically at them, like they weren't the only ones on the street.

"Hi!" piped up another voice, and then a miniature version of Tink's face appeared in another open window. "I'm Josephine! Who are you?"

"Josephine, go inside!" Tink yelled, craning her neck to look at her little sister. "They're my friends, not yours."

"That's selfish," Josephine retorted. "You're not supposed to be selfish. You're supposed to be generous." She looked back at the twins and smiled. There was a large gap where her top two teeth should have been. "Did you know that dinosaur fossils have been found on all seven continents? I can name them all."

"Dinosaurs?" Aggie asked. She had not been prepared for a mini Tink and, despite herself, smiled. She had always wanted a little sister, even if she never told her dads that. She was worried that maybe their feelings would be hurt if she mentioned it.

"Continents," Josephine said, then stuck her hands out the window and started to count on her fingers. "Africa, Antarctica—"

"Please do not encourage her," Tink said just as the opera swelled behind her. "Grandma, it's too loud! I'm going outside!"

"Australia—"

"Go watch TV with Grandma, Josephine!"

"*You* go watch TV! Europe—"

"Ugh!" Tink rolled her eyes, and then her head disappeared back into the house before the window slammed shut. Josephine was just in the middle of announcing "North America" when she also disappeared from the window with a protesting "HEY!" There was some muffled yelling before the opera music turned down, and then a shrill cry of "SOUTH AMERICA!"

And in the middle of it all, the whirligigs twirled on and on.

"Don't worry," a voice said behind them, and the girls turned to see Adriana standing behind them, her arms crossed. "It's controlled chaos."

"Are you sure about that?" Aggie said as the opera music swelled once again.

"Oh yeah, this is just what they do." Adriana was holding an aluminum bat in her hands, and she gave it a few practice swings. "Tink!" she yelled. "I've got a hard out at four thirty! Let's get this practice going! Time is money!"

Tink came storming out of the house a minute later, followed closely by her short mini me. "Hi," Tink said, looking disgusted. "My grandma said that Josephine has to play with us. I apologize in advance."

Josephine just beamed, sticking her tongue in the

space where her teeth should have been. “Hi!” she said. “I forgot the last one. Adriana!!!” She ran to the bespectacled girl, throwing her arms around her waist and giving her a hug before tilting her head up to look at her. “Did you bring me any lemonade?”

“Sorry, kid, no more freebies. I’m running a business here.” Adriana hugged her back, then looked at Tink. “Speaking of. Let’s do this. Where’s everyone else?”

Aggie could not imagine even a single new person to this chaos, but Tink gestured past them to another girl walking up the street carrying a pair of—

“Are those oven mitts?” Jac asked, squinting into the distance.

Everyone, even Josephine, groaned.

“Just don’t ask,” Tink said.

“You’ll see,” Adriana added, rolling her eyes.

“She’s allergic to *gluten*,” Josephine chimed in.

“Hi!” the girl yelled, waving one oven mitt over her head. “I just finished practice, so this is perfect.” She walked up to the twins, her long hair parted down the middle and tucked behind both ears. “I’m Marnie. It’s not a nickname or short for anything.”

“Aggie,” Aggie said, “and this is my sister, Jac.” Jac gave a wave as neither of them gave any other explanation about their own names.

“Twins,” Marnie said. “Cool.” Then she turned

toward Adriana. "My mom says she wants more coupon codes for the lemonade."

"Then you should tell her to follow us on social media," Adriana said with all the practiced cool of an experienced businesswoman. "We're giving out codes to new followers."

"You're ridiculous," Marnie said, but she didn't sound too put out. Tink was ignoring both of them and instead dragging out a bunch of equipment from their garage while Josephine did cartwheels across the front lawn. "What's up, Joey?"

"You know I don't like that name." Josephine glared while still upside down.

"Gets her every time," Marnie said with a grin. "Hey, Tink, you need help?"

"Yes, but not from you." Tink waved a hand toward Marnie, who nodded. "Josephine! Come make yourself useful!"

"Marnie's a piano player," Adriana explained as Josephine cartwheeled toward her sister. "She's like some prodigy."

Marnie just blushed and smiled, but didn't refute it, either. "I practice a lot," she said.

"One might say she's obsessed," Adriana said, nudging her friend in the ribs.

"Says the person who gave all our teachers QR codes for her lemonade stand as their end-of-the-year gift," Marnie shot back.

Adriana just shrugged and said, "Business went up by twenty percent in the third quarter," with a smile.

Aggie was starting to think that, just perhaps, she was out of her depth with this group of girls. They all seemed so . . . grown up.

And then Josephine tripped over a rock, tumbled to the ground, and let out a cry.

Five minutes and three Band-Aids later, Tink had managed to get all the softball equipment out onto the front lawn. "Okay," she said with a huff, blowing her bangs off her forehead. "Which position do you two play?"

"I basically only know how to hit the ball really far," Aggie said.

"No clue," Jac replied. "Also, wait a minute. Are we joining a team right now?"

Tink shrugged as Marnie replied, "'Team' is a little too specific a word."

"We just like to play," Tink added. "And you need a lot of people to play. It's not like badminton."

"Please do not encourage her to start a badminton team," Adriana said, then reached for a glove. "Where are Taylor and Dylan?"

"There are more of you?" Jac asked.

"Taylor is homeschooled and Dylan goes to private

school, but they should be on their way"–Tink dug her phone out of her pocket and looked at the clock–"soon." She tossed a glove at Jac. "Do you ever play first base?"

"Sure," Jac said, catching the glove in one hand.

"Is that a yes?" Tink asked.

"It's a sure," Jac replied. "Aren't all the bases exactly the same?"

Adriana, Tink, and Marnie all stared at her for a few seconds. "Oh boy," Marnie sighed.

"Maybe put her out in the outfield with Josephine," Adriana added.

"Hey!" Jac protested, knowing an insult when she heard one, even if she wasn't sure exactly why it was insulting.

"Yay!" Josephine said, and did another cartwheel to celebrate.

"First base is fine," Jac said. "I'm a quick learner."

Aggie picked up a bat and swung it a few times, trying to look like she knew what she was doing.

"Dylan!" Marnie screamed at a figure who was trudging down the street. "C'mon! We finally have eight people!"

A girl with long red hair and rainbow tie-dyed sneakers on her feet walked up to them. "Hey," she said coolly to Aggie and Jac. "Welcome to the neighborhood and all that jazz."

"Thanks," Aggie said. This girl looked oddly familiar to her, but she didn't know why. Maybe she just had one of those faces?

"Don't worry," Tink said, patting Dylan on the arm. "They're cool."

Dylan just nodded at that and went to help Marnie throw some beanbag bases into the street.

"So," Tink whispered, leaning toward Aggie and Jac like she was about to deliver state secrets. "Dylan's mom is a housewife."

Aggie blinked. "Okay," she said. "Lots of moms are?"

"No, I mean . . ." Tink widened her eyes. "A Housewife. Capital H. Like the show."

"Ohhhhh," Jac said. "Our dads love that show."

"My grandma, too," Tink whispered. "But don't tell Dylan that." She glanced back at the girl, who was now dodging playful swats from Marnie's padded oven mitts. "Her parents split up last year on the season finale. Her dad was having an affair with another capital-H Housewife and her mom found out on camera. It was a ratings bonanza." Tink paused and then added, "At least, that's what my grandma said."

Aggie looked back toward Dylan, who was smiling and seemed to pay no mind to the fact that her parents' marriage had imploded live on camera. "That's sad," Aggie said. "And mean." Next to her,

Jac nodded, and Aggie felt a small burst of warmth for her own family. Her dads may have been super dorky and did embarrassing things all the time, like when her dad would sing '80s songs at the top of his lungs while using a flower stem as a microphone, and the one time their papa tried to make up a rap to help the girls remember how to divide and multiply fractions. He got so into it that his glasses had fogged up, and he had seemed so proud of himself once he was done. (And to be fair, Aggie still found herself humming about factions, actions, and fractions from time to time.) But as embarrassing as their dads could be, she was fairly certain that neither of them wanted to split up on national television and create a ratings bonanza.

"Totally," Tink agreed with a sigh. "Anyway, just be cool with Dylan. She's kind of sensitive and stuff."

"Ow!" Marnie screamed as Dylan threw a beanbag base at her. "My hands! Watch the hands!"

"I mean, she's sensitive *most* of the time," Tink said.

"Taylor!!!" Josephine screeched, then ran toward a girl coming around the corner on her bike, one baseball glove dangling from the handlebars. As soon as she dismounted, Josephine threw her arms around her waist and Taylor hugged her back, giving her a small smile.

"So that's Taylor," Tink said. "She's our pitcher and . . . yeah. She's the best."

Taylor was quiet as she waved hello to Aggie and Jac, her eyes never quite meeting theirs. The other girls seemed to be extra affectionate toward her, with lots of pats and hair mussing. Josephine was still hanging on to her waist, and nobody called her off.

"Okay!" Adriana said. "I have a business meeting in thirty minutes, so let's do this!"

"Of course you do," Taylor said quietly even as she tugged on a glove.

"Fundraising is no joke," Adriana said. "The spreadsheets alone . . ."

"Oh, stop," Marnie said as she tugged on her oven mitts. "You love a spreadsheet."

"Do you want to *marry* a spreadsheet?" Josephine began to tease in a very woo-woo-y voice, but Tink silently pointed toward the outfield and Josephine slunk away to the neighbor's mailbox, which Aggie supposed was the stand-in for the left field line.

Adriana, meanwhile, was out at second base, slugging her fist into her glove. She looked like she knew what she was doing, which was basically the opposite of how Aggie felt. She had never actually played a game with people before. (Gym class did not count for obvious reasons.) What if she embarrassed herself? What if her home run earlier that day had been a fluke?

Aggie started to feel all tingly and hot.

"Let's gooo!" Adriana shouted. "Time is money!"

"It is not!" Tink yelled back as she took her place out in right field and Dylan meandered over behind home plate and squatted down, the perfect pose for a catcher. "Don't be such a capitalist!"

Adriana scowled and muttered something that nobody else could hear, which Aggie assumed was probably for the best.

"Let's go, Aggie! LET'S GO!" Josephine cheered from across the street. It would have been a lot more encouraging had she not been prying open the neighbor's mailbox and peering inside, rather than paying attention to what was happening.

"Josephine!" Tink yelled. "C'mon! Look alive out there!"

Josephine gave a thumbs-up in response.

Tink let out a huge sigh and shook her hair out of her face. "C'mon, Aggie! Just slug it again!"

That made Aggie think of an actual slug, which was not exactly the most encouraging thought one could have while standing at home plate. Still, she hoisted the bat up to her shoulder and kept her eye on the ball. Taylor was staring at her coolly, then drew her leg up, pulled her arm back, and sent a perfect curveball directly over the base.

Aggie swung with all her might.

And missed.

Taylor grinned. "You still got it, Tay Tay!" Tink yelled, clapping her hands together. "Two more just like that!"

"C'mon, Tay!" Marnie yelled from third base, also clapping her hands. Because of the oven mitts, though, the sound didn't have quite the same effect.

Taylor didn't acknowledge any of the comments, instead catching the ball as Dylan tossed it back to her and narrowing her eyes again, adjusting the brim of her baseball hat before winding up and throwing the ball.

This time, Aggie was prepared.

She nailed the ball high into the air, over the heads of Marnie and Tink and Taylor, directly heading for Josephine.

"Oh crap," Tink muttered. "Josephine! Heads up!"

Josephine shut the mailbox door, then looked to see the softball coming right for her. At first, Aggie was afraid that she was about to give Josephine a concussion, but she put her little gloved hand up in the air like she had been paying attention the whole time.

"I got it!" she screamed. "I got it! I got it! I— ASIA!"

The ball dropped to the ground directly next to her and began to roll into the gutter.

"I remembered the last continent!" Josephine said,

looking quite proud of herself even as the ball disappeared into the storm drain.

"Josephine!" Everyone except Jac and Aggie screamed. Aggie was too busy jogging around the "bases," making sure to tap each beanbag with a toe on her way. Jac gave her a fist bump when she cleared first base, which she appreciated. They were always on the same team, after all, even when they weren't.

"I tried my best!" Josephine yelled back.

"Did you?" Adriana sighed, putting a hand on her hip. "Don't worry, everyone, I can bring a new softball to the next practice."

Tink was still glaring at her sister. "You're getting benched!" she yelled.

"Grandma said you have to let me play with you," Josephine said back. "And it's not my fault how my memory works. Mom says I'm a unique thinker."

Marnie pulled off her oven mitts with a sigh. "I don't know how our practices can always be so eventful and yet so unproductive at the same time."

"Has this happened before?" Aggie asked as she rounded third and headed home.

"Well, there was the thing with the wasps' nest that one time," Marnie replied. "That was *definitely* eventful."

"Don't forget about when the neighbor's Pomeranian stole second base," Taylor added. "Like, literally stole the base. Have you ever seen a Pomeranian attack a beanbag? It's not pretty."

"Or environmentally friendly," Dylan said, standing up from her crouch with a sigh. "And then there was the time—"

"Tink!" a boy suddenly yelled from the front porch, holding the screen door open. He only looked a little bit older than Aggie, maybe thirteen or so. "Grandma says you have to come help make dinner!"

"Dinner!" Josephine cried, then began cartwheeling toward the house.

"Tell your girls' team to go home!" the boy added.

"Finn!" Tink yelled. "We are *gender inclusive*!"

The boy just rolled his eyes but held the door open for Josephine as she careened up the front steps and into the house, the practice a success in her mind.

Tink just sighed. "That's my dumb brother, *Phineas*," she said, emphasizing his full name in a way that Aggie knew all too well. "Ignore him. He's the worst. He's in eighth grade and he thinks he's God."

"I do not!" Finn said. "Grandma says hurry up." He glanced behind him. "Hey, Josephine, watch—" Then there was a crash followed by a muffled "Ow."

"Fine," Tink sighed, tugging off her glove and tucking it under her arm.

"It's okay," Adriana added. "I have to go prep for my meeting anyway."

"You're a workaholic," Dylan told her, but it sounded like she was teasing.

"Aggie, heads up," Marnie said, tossing her the third-base beanbag as they started to clean up the street. Aggie caught it just in time, and the girls began to empty the street.

Everyone except for Jac, who was still standing on first base, gazing toward Tink's front porch, with a look on her face that Aggie realized she had never seen on Jac's face before. It was something between wonder and happiness, and Aggie recognized it only because she felt the exact same way.

That night at dinner, their dad and papa had Questions.

"So you joined a *baseball team*?" their papa said, his fork halfway to his mouth once Aggie announced the news. "You two? Seriously?"

"We can be athletic!" Jac huffed, and Aggie nodded in solidarity. "Besides, I think it's softball."

"I remember when we tried to sign you up for soccer when you were five and you both lay down on the grass and refused to get up during the game," their dad pointed out, pushing his glasses up on his nose. "Just saying."

"We have *matured*," Aggie said primly, twirling her pasta around on her plate. "And the other girls are really nice."

"What position do you play?" their dad said, his fork still stuck in midair.

"One of the base things," Jac said.

"Oh my God," their dad murmured, and buried his face in his hands.

"First base!" Aggie said. "And I'm the hitter."

"Are you playing other teams?"

"Why are you suddenly so curious?" Jac said. "When we're in the house or on our phones, you tell us to go outside! And now that we're outside you're acting like we're international spies."

"Okay, fair, fair," their dad said, finally setting down his fork. "You've just . . . surprised us, that's all."

"Well, I think it's great," their papa said as he reached for the pepper mill. "Teamwork builds character and competition is good for the soul."

"Well, we don't play other teams," Aggie said, and she and Jac shared a look across the table that clearly said one thing: Parents. "At least, I don't *think* we play other teams. It's just, like, something fun to do."

"Tink better not make us start wearing uniforms," Jac said. "That's where I draw the line."

Their papa leaned across the table and fist-bumped her. "That's my girl."

CHAPTER 8

JAC

Jac had a lot of thoughts to sort through that night.

And most of those thoughts boiled down to one thing: *Phinneas*.

It sounded like he went by Finn, which to Jac was even better. Finn sounded like a Disney movie hero, a character in a novel, someone sure and strong. She even practiced saying it out loud, whispering it to herself after everyone had gone to bed that night, then feeling both so pleased and so embarrassed by her own self that she ducked her head into her pillow, blushing furiously.

There was absolutely no way that she was going to bring Finn up at dinner, of course. Mostly because of her dads and also a little bit (and she felt almost ashamed to admit this) because of Aggie. She knew her sister wouldn't get it, and Jac didn't feel like explaining something that she herself barely understood.

The next day at school, she made sure her outfit was on point, her shoes were tied so that she wouldn't trip and potentially humiliate herself in front of Finn, and kept an eye out for him everywhere she went.

And of course, because the world hated her, Jac didn't see him the entire day.

"How was school?" her dad asked when he picked up her and Aggie that afternoon. "Anything fun happen?"

"Oh my God, a train full of circus animals crashed into the gym," Jac said. "It was amazing."

"And then a trapeze artist swooped in while teaching us pre-algebra," Aggie added as she fastened her seat belt. "Wait until you hear about the fire-breathers."

Their dad just glared at them in the rearview mirror. "You know," he said, "I always hoped I would have creative children, and now I'm starting to regret that wish."

"Why do you always think something exciting happens at school?" Jac asked. "It's so boring. And if something exciting *does* happen, it's usually gross."

"Jenna. Fourth grade," Aggie said.

"Exactly," Jac replied.

Their dad wisely did not ask what happened to Jenna in the fourth grade.

"Okay, fine, fine," he said. "Can you tell me one good thing that happened today, at least?"

"We survived our second day of a new middle school," Aggie told him. "That's going to have to be enough for today."

Jac just nodded and didn't mention anything about Finn.

It was weird. Usually she could talk to Aggie about anything. It was like having another half of herself to discuss things with, or sort through all of her thoughts, but lately, Jac felt like they were becoming . . . different. Aggie still set up all of her stuffed animals on her bed. She didn't really care too much about clothes or shoes, even as Jac diligently unpacked and organized and reorganized her closet. And it wasn't just those things, either. Jac had tried several times to share things with Aggie, like a YouTube video about the best Korean skin care products or a listicle about the top ten ways to style your hair, but Aggie had always looked bored and uninterested, which made Jac feel strange, like Aggie was just humoring her. And deep in her heart of hearts, she wasn't sure she could talk to Aggie about the bigger things if she was already bored by the small stuff.

It made her feel like she was floating away from Aggie in a way.

But back to Finn.

Finn had very nice hair. Even shaded on the front porch, Jac had noticed that. And he had a cool T-shirt on, so points for that. Jac could always appreciate good style. But the most interesting thing about Finn was the way her stomach swooped when she thought about him, the way her chest and cheeks became warm, almost like she had a fever. It felt like the time her dad had taken them on Space Mountain at Disneyland, hurtling through the dark, scary and exciting at the same time, not knowing what was about to happen.

Jac had never felt this way before.

She both loved and hated it.

"Papa," she said the next afternoon. It was a Saturday, and they were out in the backyard. Her papa was planting an autumn vegetable bed along their fence, his brow furrowed in concentration as he worked. He was "bound and determined" to grow their own vegetables now that they finally had an outdoor space. Jac and Aggie, on the other hand, had their doubts. Jac hadn't known it was possible to kill a cactus, but their papa had managed to do it. "That's why I married a florist," he would always say. "Someone has to keep the plants alive."

"Yeah, bug?" her papa said, digging a hole and pouring a few seedlings into the dirt. Jac said a quick prayer of hope for them. "What's up?"

Jac dug her own hole, liking the feeling of dirt under her nails. It smelled like sun and water and soil, all good things to grow. "How did you know that you liked Dad?"

Her papa looked over at her, but before he could say anything, a voice yelled from inside the house. "My sparkling personality!" her dad called.

"Oh, brother," her papa said.

"My sharp jawline and devastatingly handsome face!"

Jac giggled.

"My ability to juggle!"

Her papa rolled his eyes and looked back at Jac. "His humility," he whispered, which made Jac laugh even harder. "His subtlety. The fact that he never remembers where he puts his glasses."

"No, but seriously," Jac said, then poured her own packet of seedlings into the dirt.

"Why do you ask, bug?"

Her parents were the only people ever allowed to call her "bug." Jac would never admit it out loud, but it made her feel warm and safe, like it was one thing that would never change even when it felt like so much was changing.

"I don't know," she said, trying to sound as casual as possible. "I was just thinking about it."

"Okay," her papa said. He was still digging at the dirt, but Jac noticed he hadn't moved down the line to a new spot. "Well, I liked—and like—your dad for a lot of reasons. I guess it wasn't just one thing; it was just the overall package. Does that make sense? I knew he was a good person, that he'd be a good partner and dad."

Jac nodded, gently tapping the dirt over the seeds. "Grow strong," she told them, then dug a new hole. "But like, how did you *know*?"

Her papa sat back and adjusted his hat. "I just did," he said. "I could feel it." He paused before adding, "Is there someone that you have feelings for?"

"Barf," Jac said automatically, even as the tips of her ears started to burn. She hoped it would just look like she had been out in the sun for too long. "No. Gross."

Her papa smiled. "It's okay if you like someone," he said. "And it's okay to not want to talk about it, either."

Her dad appeared at the back door. "What did he tell you?" he asked. "Did he tell you that he was thirty minutes late to our first date? Hmm? Did he mention *that* part?"

Jac looked at her papa. "That is terrible," she said. "Rude."

"Mm-hmm," her dad said, but he looked more fond than annoyed.

"I told you, there was *traffic*!"

"If I had a nickel for every time I've heard that excuse. Hey, Jac Jac, can you go get your sister? Is she at Tink's?"

Jac groaned inwardly. Her parents had a "no cell phones on the weekend" family rule, which made things annoying and complicated. (Especially because she was pretty sure they were sneaking their own phones after she and Aggie went to bed.) "Can I just text her, please?" she said. "Or just, like, yell down the street like they did in the olden days?"

"Nice try," her dad said.

Jac sighed, then set down her trowel and got to her feet. "Tell my seeds I loved them," she said to her papa.

"Will do," he replied. "And tell your dad—"

"Tell your papa . . ." her other dad started to respond, but even as Jac headed toward the front door, she could hear them dissolving into laughter, and she hightailed it out of there before (the horror) she could see them start to kiss.

She went around the corner to Tink's house, where she could hear the TV blaring even before she got to the front porch. Tink's grandmother wore hearing aids only when her family forced her to, which meant that otherwise the TV was turned up to the full volume and everyone had to yell so she could hear them. "She's stubborn." Tink had shrugged, and Jac couldn't judge that. She could only hope that when she was an old lady, she'd be as stubborn then as she was now.

When Aggie had left that morning, she had said that Tink needed help setting up a practice schedule and also keeping an eye on Josephine, since Finn was going to some all-day soccer camp thing and her mom had to go into the office. "Better you than me," Jac had said breezily.

"Yeah, no kidding," Aggie had replied.

And on her way to fetch her sister, Jac hadn't thought about the possibility that Finn was at home. She imagined him at soccer camp, running around on the field and doing . . . whatever soccer players did. She hadn't even considered it, which is why she hadn't brushed her hair or changed out of her dirt-stained shirt or scrubbed under her nails or done anything—anything at all!—to make herself look somewhat presentable.

Which was a real bummer for Jac, because Finn answered the door.

He was holding a bottle of red Gatorade and wearing a grass-stained shirt, his hair brushed off his forehead. "Hey," he said. "The other one of you is here."

"I know!" Jac said, smiling brightly even though

her heart was pounding. She wasn't used to being out of her depths, wasn't used to being thrown off her game. She didn't like it. "That's so cool."

"Jac!" a voice screamed from inside, and Jac sighed inwardly.

"Hi, Josephine," she said.

"Did you know that penguins don't have teeth?" Josephine came up to the door and wrapped her arms around her big brother's waist. He grimaced but made no attempts to shake her off, which made Jac feel warm all over.

"I did not," Jac said.

"Nobody knows that fact except for geeks like you," Finn added, and Josephine half-heartedly punched him in the arm while trying to disentangle herself from him.

"Can you tell Aggie that she needs to come home?"

"Tell her yourself," Finn said, holding open the screen door and standing back so Jac should come in.

Was a boy inviting her into his house? Was this okay? Did this count as something? Jac didn't even know what it would count as, definitely not a date.

Right? Ugh, Jac would happily toss her heart into the garbage disposal if it meant she didn't have to feel as twisted up as she did right then.

Josephine let go of her brother's waist long enough to latch onto Jac. "You smell good," she said, then let go of her and ran off upstairs. "AGGGIIIEEEEEEE!" she yelled. "You have to leave now!"

The sound of the TV was in the background, but Jac couldn't see Tink's grandmother anywhere, which meant that it was just her and Finn.

Alone.

Together.

"Cool," Jac said, even though Finn hadn't said anything.

"Yeah," he said. "Nice shoes."

Jac was never taking these shoes off ever again. Bury her in them when she's a hundred years old.

"Thanks," she managed to say. "Nice . . . hair."

Finn paused for a second. "Thanks?" he said.

"No problem," she replied, and prayed for an earthquake to hit right that second so that the ground would open up and swallow her whole, shoes and all.

"Here she is!" Josephine yelled as she came thundering back down the stairs, Aggie and Tink close on her heels.

"I just texted you the practice schedule," Tink said. "Do you know how hard it is to coordinate seven—"

"Eight! Did you know that there are eighteen different kinds of penguins?" Guess who.

Tink sighed. "Eight people's schedules."

Josephine dangled off the banister, a huge grin on her face. "I am *always* available to practice."

Jac just nodded, still smarting from her dumb comment about Finn's hair. (It *was* nice hair, though.) "We're not allowed to use our phones on weekends," Jac said instead. "Family rule."

"Yeah, that's what Ag said. Sucks."

"Dads said you have to come home and help with dinner," Jac said, and Aggie went to find her shoes in the pile by the front door.

"It's lasagna night," Aggie explained to them as she tugged on her slip-on Vans. Jac couldn't help but notice that Finn didn't compliment her shoes. "My dad gets squicked out by the wet noodles, so I have to help him."

"Delish," Tink said. "Have fun! And don't forget, practice on Tuesday!"

"I'll text you back as soon as I get my phone," Aggie promised. "Bye, Finn, bye, Josephine." Then she leaned back and looked up the stairs. "Bye, Mrs. Alvarez!"

"Bye!" called a voice before the TV turned up a notch.

"Bye," Jac said, talking to everyone but looking at Finn.

"Later," Finn said, going to shut the door behind them.

"Did you know that a polar bear can eat—" Josephine started to yell before the door shut behind them.

"I wouldn't get too attached to the polar bears if

I were Josephine," Jac said as they started to trudge home.

"Aw, that's sad," Aggie said. "I'm rooting for the polar bears."

And after a minute of silence between them, Aggie stopped her pace. "You're being weird," she said.

"I haven't even said anything!" Jac protested. "How am I being weird?"

"I don't know, just your whole aura." Aggie narrowed her eyes at her sister. "Did you sneak your phone out? Do you have it now?"

"No!" Jac said. "I came to get you and now we're going home so you can help make the squicky lasagna." She nudged her sister's arm. "You're the one being the weirdo." Privately, though, she burned inside.

Sometimes it seemed like Aggie knew Jac better than she knew herself.

On Monday, leftover squicky lasagna consumed again the night before, Jac got ready for school the same way some people prepared for prom. She got up early to make sure her hair looked at least semi-presentable, she fixed a few chips in her nail polish and checked her teeth three times to make sure they didn't have lip gloss on them, and she even steamed a wrinkle out of her shirt.

Aggie, who looked like she had rolled out of bed

and been taken hostage, glanced at her in the car. "Why do you look so nice?"

"Thanks," Jac said. "I'll take it as a compliment."

"Sorry. You know I'm cranky in the morning."

"I know," Jac replied. "It's cool." But she was thrumming inside, both nervous and anxious to get to school and look for Finn again. As soon as their dad dropped them off, she nearly sprinted up the steps to her locker, leaving Aggie behind as she caught up with Marnie. (It was weird to see Marnie not wearing her oven mitts.)

Her locker lock was reliably useless, and she had to spin the combo three times in a row before it would finally open, leaving her irritated and killing a little bit of her new-crush buzz. "Finally," she muttered as she finally wedged it open, switching out her ridiculously heavy textbooks, and then made sure to fluff her hair a little in the tiny mirror she had put up before shutting the door.

Across the way, three girls were giggling behind their hands, and when Jac looked over at them, they pointedly looked back at her. One of them was in her pre-algebra class, but she didn't recognize the other two. They looked older than her, though, and definitely taller.

More of her new-crush buzz slipped away.

"Hey, *Jacaranda*," one of them said, and Jac felt

a little shiver up her spine. No one ever used her full name unless (A) she was in trouble or (B) they wanted to get a rise out of her. Even her grandma Lydia, who once gave them etiquette books for their birthdays, called her Jac.

"Hey," she said carefully, kind of feeling like someone had handed her a grenade with the pin pulled out.

"Nice shoes," another girl said, and as they started to walk away, one of them bumped her shoulder in a way that could have seemed accidental to anyone else watching.

Jac knew that it was very much not accidental.

And what was wrong with her shoes? They were her favorite red high-top sneakers! She glanced around the halls and saw that most of the other kids had white sneakers or Birkenstocks or Vans.

"Hey!" Aggie called out, and Jac looked up, suddenly very relieved and grateful to see the most familiar face on the planet. "You dork, you put your math homework in my bag." She shook her head as she pulled it out, handing it to her sister.

"Thanks," Jac said.

"Are you okay? You look like you have a fever. Please don't get sick because when you get sick, *I* get sick and—"

"I'm fine," Jac replied before her sister could go into an anxiety spiral that had both of them on their deathbeds. "It's just hot out today."

Marnie caught up to them, chattering away about her latest trip to the orthodontist and how awful it had been, and as she and Aggie fell into step, Jac let herself drift back. A brand-new worry had taken hold in her stomach and she didn't like it.

She didn't like it at all.

Later that afternoon, Jac and her dad were once again in the back yard, weeding around the roses and dodging thorns. Jac thought about bringing up the incident to him, but she already knew what he would say, knew what her parents would do. "They can tell you're an individual," they would have reassured her, using one of their all-time favorite adjectives. "You're *independent*." A close second.

And then they would probably set up a meeting with the principal, and Jac would sooner lie down in the middle of the road and have a truck run her over than let that happen. There would probably be some emergency anti-bullying assembly, everyone would have to sign a contract stating that they wouldn't be mean to one another, or something equally terrible like that. And then those girls would know that Jac had told someone, had made it a bigger deal than it was, and things would only get worse from there.

A Subaru suddenly pulled up to the front curb, interrupting Jac's worrying, and a dark head of hair popped out the passenger window. "Hey!" Adriana yelled, waving. "Do you want to go to the hospital?"

Jac and her dad both looked up. "Uh," Jac said. "That's our friend Adriana."

Her dad frowned under the brim of his Giants baseball hat. "Any idea why she wants to take you to the hospital?"

"Great question."

"Sorry!" Adriana said. "I mean, do you want to come to the children's hospital with me? I'm donating a bunch of stuff that we bought with the lemonade-stand money."

"Context is so important!" laughed the woman behind the wheel. She had dark brown hair and seemed bemused by Adriana's urgency. "Hi, I'm Adri's mom. She hasn't stopped talking about Aggie and Jac all weekend!"

"Mooooom!" Adriana said. "Oh my God."

Jac just grinned. "Hi, Mrs. Gutierrez. Can I go?" she asked her dad.

She and her dad went down to the car so that Adri's mom and her dad could do what Jac and Aggie called "the parent dance": introduction, jokes about their kids, talking about where they live, lots of smiling.

"She is so embarrassing," Adriana muttered to Jac as her mom started to tell Jac's dad about the best coffee places in the neighborhood. "I just said that identical twins joined our team."

"No worries," Jac said. "And if my dad says I can go, I'll go." She gestured down to her dirt-covered hands and knees. "I just have to change."

"Cool. Is Aggie home? She can come, too, if she wants."

"Yeah, but she's working on some diorama for her art class." That was an understatement, but Jac didn't feel like getting into the details about how Aggie and their papa were trying to wire a shoebox with electricity, which was part of the reason why Jac and her dad had escaped outside. "Dad, can I go?"

Ten minutes and parental permission later, Jac was riding in the back seat next to Adriana, who had moved from her seat up front. "So we went yesterday and bought all this stuff because our earnings in Q2 were higher than we thought they were going to be." Adriana pulled out an iPad and opened a spreadsheet, then pointed to a number. "See?"

"Wow," Jac said. She hadn't ever known someone her age who could earn that much money. "What do you do with the rest of it?"

Adriana blinked at her. "What do you mean, the rest of it?"

"Like, do you pay yourself or . . . ?"

"No, it all goes to the children's hospital," she said. "That's why I have the stand. We buy supplies, but that's it. I donate the rest of it."

Jac immediately decided that she needed to up her "being a good person" game, stat.

When they got to the hospital, Adriana's mom hopped out of the car and went to open the trunk. "Adri, why don't you go inside and let the front desk know that we're here?"

Adriana nodded as she clicked out of her seat belt, Jac following her lead into the air-conditioned lobby of the hospital. It was light and airy and felt a lot less scary than how she thought a hospital might feel, especially one for kids, but Adriana seemed unfazed, like she had done this a million times before.

"Hi," Adriana said breezily, pushing her sunglasses on top of her head and smiling at the receptionist. "I'm Adriana. I own the Handing You Lemons lemonade stand. Maybe you've seen our social media platforms?" She passed the woman a business card. Jac wondered if she had them in every single pocket of her clothes. "We're here to drop off some supplies. I think Lisa is expecting us."

Jac had often considered herself mature, maybe even *cool* if she was being super generous with herself, but Adriana was like a grown-up. It blew her mind. Jac didn't even want to call someone on the phone, much less talk to a *stranger*! In *person*! In a *hospital*!

The receptionist started to dial a number, and

Adriana turned back to Jac and smiled. "I've been working with Lisa for two years," she said. "She's the best. She sends us a wish list every year, and we do our best to get everything on it."

"I thought you just made *lemonade*," Jac said. "This is amazing. You're like a real adult."

Adriana rolled her eyes. "Whatever. I only started it because of my older brother. He died before I was born, he was only a few months old, so I didn't even know him, but this kind of makes me feel closer to him, you know? Like he would approve."

Jac tried not to look as shocked as she felt. She couldn't imagine a world without Aggie. Even when she wanted to throttle her twin sister, she still needed her.

"It's okay," Adriana added before Jac could say anything. "I'm not like super sad about it. It was a long time ago. But I think it helps my mom and dad, too." She shrugged and looked out to the front of the hospital, where her mom was unloading the car, pulling out supplies with amazing speed. It was clear they had this operation down to a science. "They don't really talk about it, but I can tell." She smiled at Jac again. "So is it weird being a twin?"

"Sometimes," Jac said with a laugh. "It's weird when there's someone else that looks exactly like you. It's like you're an individual but not really."

Adriana let out a loud guffaw at that, right as Lisa came down to meet them, along with a few people pushing hand trucks. "Hey," Adriana said as they hugged. "You're in luck. Business is booming this year."

It took three trips for all of them to get everything upstairs in the elevators, and by the time they were done, Jac felt a little sweaty and a lot relieved that they were done. "I think you earned yourselves Slurpees," Adriana's mom said as they climbed back into the car, the air-conditioning blasting. "Jac, are you a red or blue Slurpee person?"

"Red," Jac said immediately. "Aggie's the blue twin."

"Maybe we should introduce a special limited-edition lemonade slushie," Adriana said, and was already pulling out her iPad before they had even left the parking lot.

After they were back in the car, Slurpees in hand and Adriana's mom talking to someone on Bluetooth, Jac decided to take a leap of faith.

"So," she said, casually, so, so casually. "Finn seems kind of cool."

Adriana glanced at her. "You mean Tink's brother? That mouth breather?"

Jac frowned and gently kicked at her leg. "He is *not*," she said.

"No, he's not. I'm only teasing." Adriana took another long swig of her drink. "It's just that I've known him for years at this point. He's, I don't know. He's Finn."

"Does he ever, like, do anything?" Jac asked. "Like hobbies? Or sports, maybe?"

Adriana side-eyed her. "Do you like *Finn*?"

"No!" Jac squealed. "Oh my God, no!" She did, she so did. "It's just that . . . I don't know, he has nice hair."

Adriana wiggled her eyebrows. "Mm-hmm. Nice hair. Okay."

Jac pretended that the heat in her cheeks was from the late-summer sun and not the burning embarrassment she felt at being found out.

"Relax," Adriana said. "Finn's cool. You could definitely do a lot worse. What did Aggie say when you told her?"

"She, um . . . I haven't really mentioned anything like . . ." Jac distracted herself by using the spoon end of her straw to get the last remaining part of her drink.

"Got it," Adriana said. "This is top secret. No worries."

"I mean, it's not like it's *super* secret or anything." Had she ever kept anything from Aggie before? Maybe this was a bad idea to talk to Adriana. What if Aggie found out? Would she feel betrayed? Hurt?

Clearly she had picked up on Aggie's bad habit of worrying everything to death.

"It's just that I'm still figuring out how I feel," Jac amended, adjusting her sunglasses over her eyes. *Cool dispassion.* "I think I need to keep my options open."

"Awesome," Adriana said, clinking her empty cup against Jac's. "You're a modern woman. You don't need to be tied down."

Her mother laughed from the front seat. "You two back there talking like you're thirty-year-olds."

Adriana caught Jac's eye and made the universal face for *What do parents know?* and Jac laughed.

That night, Jac poked her head into Aggie's room. The shoebox had not, thankfully, burst into flames at any point during the day, and now Aggie had a very realistic diorama of a lakeside evening, complete with fireflies. "Hey, nerd," Jac said.

"Hey, dork," Aggie replied without looking up from her iPad.

"What are you doing?"

"Trying to find realistic cricket noises online." She glanced up. "How was Adri?"

"Very driven and a little intimidating," Jac said, then flopped onto Aggie's bed. It was perfectly made, unlike Jac's own bed, which made it perfect for flopping.

Aggie waved a hand at her but didn't look up from her research. "Ugh, you're getting your Jac germs all over my bed."

Jac rolled around a little bit just because she could. "Hey," she said.

"What?"

"You know that I'd, like, totally lose it if we weren't sisters."

Aggie's head came flying up. "Why wouldn't we be sisters?"

"I just mean, like, if anything happened to you."

"What?! Did you overhear something? What's going to happen to me?"

"Nothing!" Jac said. This was not going according to plan at all. "I just mean that you're my sister and I love you."

Aggie shook her head at her. "You really need to work on your delivery," she said, but she looked relieved. "And I love you, too. Weirdo."

"You'd probably have better luck with frog sounds," Jac said, coming over to sit on Aggie's desk now that her bed had been thoroughly mussed up. "Here, let me help."

And Aggie scooted over and let her.

CHAPTER 9

AGGIE

"OKAY OKAY OKAY BATTER UP!"

Aggie winced as Tink screamed less than three feet from her ear. "Tink," she said.

"Sorry, sorry." Tink smiled and held up her hands. "You know me—I just get competitive."

"Against *who*?" Dylan said from her catcher's crouch. "We're all on the same team!"

"It's the principle of competition," Tink started to say, but Dylan held up her hand.

"I don't want to hear the 'principle of competition' speech again," she said. "I could recite it in my sleep at this point."

Tink just looked at Aggie and beamed. "It's pretty memorable." But behind her, Dylan made cut-throat motions, a clear warning to not pursue it further.

Which was fine by Aggie.

"Who's next?" Tink yelled, and then groaned as Josephine swaggered up to the plate, swinging a bat that was more than half her size.

"BATTER UP!" Josephine cried, grinning wildly and looking more and more like her sister with every passing step.

"Let's go, Josephine!" Jac called from her spot at first base, clapping her hands together. She was wearing flavored lip gloss and a skort, her hair pulled back from her face with a flowery headband. She looked, in a word, dressed up, and Aggie was suspicious. "We're going to play baseball in the street," she had said as they walked toward Tink's house.

"You never know what could happen," Jac had just said. "I like to look nice sometimes. So sue me." Which was exactly the kind of vague response from her sister that drove Aggie up a wall sometimes. It was like Jac knew something she didn't know, and the less Aggie knew, the more Jac enjoyed the mystery.

Aggie loved her sister with her whole heart, but she wondered what sort of bliss Taylor, an only child, enjoyed on a daily basis.

Taylor was on the pitcher's mound now, her hat once again pulled low over her eyes as Dylan shuffled around behind Josephine. Taylor took a few steps closer toward Josephine, who frowned and thrust her arm out in front of her. "No, Taylor!" she said. "Don't get closer! I'm seven—I'm not a baby!"

Taylor sighed and took a few steps backward.

Josephine smiled to herself, but as soon as she hoisted the bat up to her shoulder, she frowned again. "CAR!"

They all automatically scattered. The rules on "CAR!" had been established a long time ago: everyone got out of the way as quickly as possible, and everyone was responsible for their position, which meant that all the people on base had to drag the beanbags out of the way. Jac grabbed her base and hauled it over to the sidewalk, as did Adriana and Marnie; Aggie herded up the spare bats; and Dylan grabbed Josephine's hand to make sure that she didn't dawdle before they were all taken out by someone's Range Rover.

They all stood on the side of the road, waiting for the stream of cars to die down, and then went back to their positions. "It's still my turn!" Josephine cried.

"Nobody said it wasn't," Tink muttered as Aggie watched Jac reapply her lip gloss and then tuck it back into her pocket before patting her hair down and glancing toward Tink's house.

"BATTER UP!" Josephine yelled again. Over on third base, Marnie's hands were moving up and down on an invisible keyboard, her fingers twitching inside her oven mitts.

"Marnie!" Tink shouted. "This is softball practice, not piano practice!"

"I have a recital next Sunday!" Marnie said. "I have to practice even when I'm not practicing!"

Tink rolled her eyes but let it go. "Okay, everyone, heads up, look alive and—"

"CAR!" Adriana cried.

"Oh for Pete's sake," Dylan muttered, grabbing Josephine again.

"Why are all these cars coming through here?" Tink complained as the eight of them stood on the sidewalk, watching a steady stream of electric cars and SUVs slowly crawling down their street. "We never get traffic like this! They're interrupting practice!"

Adriana held up her phone. "Waze."

Tink let out a huffy breath. *"Waze,"* she replied, like she was naming a mortal enemy.

Adriana shifted slightly next to them, and Aggie could see her mouth twitching a little, probably imagining how much lemonade she could be selling to everyone stuck in this new stream of traffic.

"Hi!" Josephine said brightly, waving at a car as it passed.

"Don't you think," Adriana started to say, "that they look . . . a little . . . thirsty?"

Tink shot her a dirty look.

"I'm just saying!" Adriana added.

Tink threw her hands up in the air. "Fine," she muttered. "Go get your stand. Practice is done."

Josephine froze, and Aggie was fairly certain that she saw her lower lip tremble a little bit. "But it was my turn!" she protested. "I never get to bat!"

So Taylor and Dylan pulled her over to the front yard and did a few minutes of batting practice with her. "It's not the same," Josephine pouted, but then she hit the ball and Taylor fumbled it, so she was all smiles again.

Meanwhile, Adriana's mom pulled up in their car after several urgent texts from her daughter, and Adriana got to work expertly setting up her stand. Aggie helped her put up a small billboard while Marnie put out cups and Tink sulked on the sidewalk. "We could be practicing right now," she said, her pout looking a lot like Josephine's.

Jac patted her arm. "Just let Adri do her thing," she said. "It's for a good cause."

That seemed to mollify Tink somewhat, or at least enough that she begrudgingly helped Adri stack some business cards. Josephine, emboldened by her one chance at bat, started yelling, "It's organic!!" at the passing cars. Aggie wasn't sure if that was helping or not, but it seemed to keep her busy.

"She's obsessed with this stand," Taylor said as

she came up next to Aggie. "She'll probably end up on *Shark Tank* one day."

"As one of the sharks," Aggie said, which made Taylor laugh.

"Anyway, it's probably for the best," Taylor said. "I mean that practice got cut short. My dad's taking me to the library so I can get a book for my English class. I have to read the first two chapters by tomorrow."

"Which book?" Aggie asked.

"The Book Thief?" Taylor said. "Have you read it?"

"I read it last year in school," Aggie said. "You can borrow my copy if you want. Come on over—it's annotated and everything."

So Aggie and Taylor got ready to go back to Aggie's house, with Jac opting to stay behind and help Adriana with her lemonade stand. "Tell Papa I'll be home in an hour," Jac said. "Unless sales go through the roof, of course."

Adriana, who was busy serving a cup of lemonade through the window of a Prius under her mom's watchful eye, held up two crossed fingers.

Aggie wasn't quite sure why Jac was suddenly so invested in Adri's lemonade stand, but she didn't stay to question it. Taylor was already dusting herself off and tucking her pitcher's glove back into her backpack, so Aggie scooped up her own bag and started to lead Taylor to her house.

"So is it weird moving to a new city?" Taylor asked

as they walked, expertly kicking a stone a few feet ahead of them, then kicking it again when they got closer.

"It's not weird, it's just . . ." Aggie shrugged. "I don't know. Different. Like when you get new shoes, you know? They feel really stiff and strange at first. It takes a while to break them in."

Taylor smiled. "That's a really great way to describe it."

"My dad tells me that I have a very vivid imagination," Aggie said with a grin. "But I don't always think that's a compliment."

When they got to the house, Aggie's papa was at the kitchen table, frowning at something on his laptop. "Hi, this is Taylor," Aggie said, dropping her bag in the front hallway. "She's borrowing a book. Can we have a snack?"

"Hey, Taylor," her papa said. He did something with money and other people's money and always looked stressed whenever he was working, even though he swore up and down that he liked his job. "Does your parental person know you're here?"

Taylor held up her phone. "I just texted my dad. He's going to pick me up at four."

"Then yes, but Aggie, take your bag . . . ?"

"Upstairs," Aggie said, barely resisting the urge to roll her eyes.

Her papa nodded. "Excellent."

"He's so predictable," Aggie said as soon as she and Taylor were upstairs. "He acts like my backpack is going to set the whole downstairs on fire if it's on the floor for more than five seconds."

"My mom's the same way," Taylor said, looking around at Aggie's room. "Cool room. It's very . . . neat."

"Thanks," Aggie said, preening a little. She took a lot of pride in her neatness. "It took me two whole days to unpack. I think Jac's still living out of boxes, though. We're really different like that."

"Does everyone expect you to be, like, the same person?" Taylor said, giving Aggie's stuffed animals little pats on the head.

"Sometimes?" Aggie said, sitting down on the bed. "But only if they don't really know us."

"Yeah, you look alike, but that's kind of it," Taylor agreed. "Even your voices sound different sometimes."

Aggie wisely decided not to mention two summers ago, when she spent two whole months speaking with a British accent in an effort to not sound so much like Jac. "You sound like Mary Poppins," her dad had finally told her. "And I'm pretty sure no actual British person says 'Pip pip, cheerio' anymore."

"Ta," Jac had added, where she was glaring at Aggie from the couch.

So it had been a short-lived experiment.

"Yeah, we do sound different sometimes" was all Aggie said instead. "So how did you meet Tink if you're homeschooled?"

Taylor, who had been running her finger along the spines on Aggie's bookshelf, stopped right at Aggie's copy of *Brown Girl Dreaming*. "Did . . . did no one tell you?"

Aggie's interest was definitely piqued.

"Um, I don't think so, but I also don't know what we're talking about, so . . . maybe?"

Taylor smiled at that and turned back to Aggie's bookshelf, not replying, and Aggie got the feeling that she needed to put the conversation in a different direction as fast as possible. "Hey, do you want to go put our feet in the pool?" she said. "We've got some time before your mom gets here, and it's so hot out. I feel like even my ankles are sweating."

"Sure," Taylor said. "That's awesome that you have a pool."

They ran down the stairs on each other's heels. Then Aggie pointed Taylor in the direction of the kitchen. "There are fruit snacks in the pantry," she said. "Grab some? I'm just going to tell my dad that we'll be outside."

Taylor nodded and disappeared as Aggie went back down the hall, knocking on her papa's closed door. "Papa?" she said.

There was a brief pause before her papa wheeled over and opened the door. He had headphones on that made him look like an air traffic controller. "Aggs," he said. "I'm on a really important Zoom. What is it?"

"Can Taylor and I go outside and put our feet in the pool?"

"Does Taylor know how to swim?"

Aggie paused, then leaned out of the doorway toward the kitchen. "Taylor!" she yelled. "Do you know how to swim?!"

"Yeah!" came the shout back.

"Aggie." Her papa blinked very, very slowly. "Next time just go ask, okay?"

"Can we, though? Go outside?"

"Yes, but stay near the shallow end so I can see you from the window."

"Thanks!" Aggie cried, then made sure to not slam the office door too hard behind her.

Once they were outside, Aggie and Taylor shucked off their sandals and immediately stuck their feet in the cool blue water. "Ahh," Aggie said. "Better than air-conditioning. I like your nail polish."

Taylor smiled as she lifted one foot out of the water. "Thanks. My mom and I got pedicures last week."

"Cool," Aggie said, even though she'd rather do math homework than let a stranger touch her bare feet.

“I, um.” Taylor cleared her throat and started again. “I’m sorry if I got weird upstairs.”

“That’s okay,” Aggie said. “I’m sorry if I asked a personal question.”

“No, it’s not that,” Taylor said, then took a deep breath. “It’s just that I don’t really have to tell many people about it since everyone around here has known each other forever.”

Aggie turned her ankles around in one direction, then the other. “Well, you can tell me whatever you want,” she said. “Or not.”

“When you asked how I met Tink, it’s because I got kicked off my Little League team,” Taylor said. “And someone told me that there was this girl a few blocks away who had this, like, not quite official team with all these other kids who, for whatever reason, couldn’t or didn’t want to play on an actual team. And then, a couple of days later, she and Josephine showed up at my door and said they needed a pitcher.” Taylor shrugged. “So here I am.”

“Why’d you get kicked off your team?” Aggie asked. “You seem pretty nice, not like a cheater or anything.”

Taylor smiled a little, but it was more sad than happy. “Because I’m trans,” she said softly. “And I had been playing for a really long time on a boys’ Little League team and some of the other parents didn’t like that very much. But then a while ago, the girls' team wouldn't let me play on their team, either. The other players didn't really care, but some of the moms and dads got really upset and then the league got involved and there was a big meeting and sooooo yeah. Here we are."

"Why do they even care?" Aggie said, already feeling herself getting heated. She hated when grown-ups were jerks. It just felt so unfair that kids were expected to be perfect all the time and then adults could go and hurt someone's feelings—especially a kid's feelings—just because they felt like it. "Why is it any of their business?"

Taylor shrugged. "I don't know. Parents can be really weird sometimes. Not mine—they were great. They *are* great. But . . . yeah." Taylor trailed her hand in the pool water. "I just like playing baseball, you know? And Tink and everyone else let me do that and don't act like it's a big deal."

"Because it's *not* a big deal," Aggie said. "Seriously. Who cares? You're a nice person. You always pitch *really* slow to Josephine so that she can hit the ball."

Taylor smiled at that. "Josephine," she said fondly. "She's either going to be president or an international jewel thief. But Tink's whole family was really nice to me and my mom and dad after, you know, a bunch of other people weren't so nice. . . ." She trailed off.

"They invited us over for dinner. Her grandma sent us home with a bunch of desserts. It really meant a lot. Finn even offered to beat someone up for me, but he was kidding." She paused. "I think."

Aggie thought about Tink, how she was always cheering everyone on, how she never left anyone behind, and she felt a surge of pride for her friend.

"But that's why my mom thought maybe we'd do homeschooling for a year, just so things could calm down," Taylor continued. "And I really didn't need another round of meetings where all the adults talk about which bathroom I should use."

Aggie gasped. *"No."*

Taylor glanced up. "Yep."

Aggie sighed and flopped back down on her bed. "Adults are so rude," she said. "They always make a big deal out of nothing, and then the little things?" She mimed an explosion with her hands. "You can use any of our bathrooms any time you want. Use all of them!"

Taylor's smile got a bit wider. "Okay."

"And don't worry, you don't need Finn. Jac will definitely beat someone up if you need her to. When we were in kindergarten, she dumped a bunch of paint on a boy because he made fun of me for not being able to say my *r*'s. She's annoying, but she's *very* loyal." Aggie could still see the blue paint dripping off the boy's sneakers, the tears streaking down his cheeks and the triumphant look on Jac's face.

"Sometimes I wish I had a sister, like you have Jac," Taylor said, flopping down next to Aggie. "You'll always have a friend."

"Well, you have new friends now. *Good* friends. And it's okay to expect your friends to show up for you. That's what friends do, right? They show up for one another. They're a . . . Wait for it." She paused a bit and then wiggled her eyebrows dramatically. "They're a *team*."

Taylor burst out laughing and gave Aggie's shoulder a shove. "That is so cheesy!"

"It's an inherited trait," Aggie said, even though she was giggling, too. "And trust me, you can borrow Jac *whenever* you want. No late fees."

"Jac's really cool," Taylor said, and Aggie was very grateful that her sister wasn't around to hear that compliment. Her head would probably explode with joy.

"Yeah, well, sometimes she's just really annoying. Like lately, she's always doing her hair and putting on lip gloss every five minutes and moisturizing." Aggie rolled her eyes. "She thinks she's practically a teenager now."

"I like lip gloss," Taylor said. "It's not the worst thing."

"No, it's just the *way* she does it." Aggie could feel herself getting annoyed thinking about it, the way Jac had started hogging the bathroom mirror when Aggie only needed to brush her teeth or wash her hands or something. "So yeah, having a sister isn't all roses. Just so you know."

"Noted," Taylor said, then smoothed down her hair before readjusting her hat. "Thanks for being cool about all this. I'm not used to having to tell people about it. Most everyone here already knows or somebody else already told them."

Aggie shrugged. "No biggie," she said. "My dads had friends back in San Francisco that were trans, and they were awesome." She missed Linda and Henry sometimes, how they would always bring over the best gifts for her and Jac when they were younger, like a wand filled with glitter and a 3D mini puzzle of the Eiffel Tower. "Nobody cared, or at least we didn't."

"Are people ever weird with you because you have two dads?" Taylor asked.

"Not really," Aggie said "Like, sometimes someone will say 'Where's your mom?' if we're at the airport flying somewhere, but that's about it. Mostly just weird stuff that people say without thinking." She shrugged. "But I say weird stuff sometimes, too, so it all balances out."

Taylor laughed at that. "Fair enough," she said.

She dug her phone out of her bag and looked at the time. "I think I need to get going. My dad's going to be here soon."

Aggie nodded and started to draw her feet out of the water.

Taylor stood up and stretched a little. "Thanks, Aggie. For the book, I mean."

"Oh, sure," Aggie said. "You don't have to even give it back. I think Jac has her own copy, too. It's really good. The narrator"—she paused dramatically—"is Death. The Grim Reaper."

"Cool," Taylor said. "That's awesome."

Aggie nodded. "I thought you'd appreciate that." She hesitated before adding, "Is it okay if I tell Jac?"

"Sure," Taylor said, shrugging a little. "She'll find out eventually anyway, and it's not like it's a secret or anything. And like I said, Jac's cool."

After Taylor's dad picked her up, Aggie wandered back downstairs, her mind feeling too swimmy with thoughts to focus on her homework or YouTube or anything else to entertain her.

Her papa was still on his laptop, tapping away at something that seemed important, but at least his door was open. "Hi," Aggie said, draping herself over his back and pressing her chin into his shoulder. "Are you done Zooming?"

"Hey, kiddo," he said without looking up from his

computer. "Yep. What's the haps? Did Taylor's dad pick her up?"

"Yeah," Aggie said. "I'm glad she's my friend. She seems really nice."

"Well, I'm glad you and Jac are making friends. What's her name, Tink, and whoever else is in that ragamuffin crew of yours."

Aggie giggled. "They have *names*, Papa."

"Of course they do. Let me see, there's Hortense, Petunia, Bertha, and that little one who's always talking about penguins every time she comes over. . . ."

"Papa!" Aggie protested. "That's Josephine. But yeah, you're right about the penguins. She's obsessed. What are you working on?"

"Oh, Dad and I are just going to a meeting later this week for the neighborhood. Something about fire roads and evacuation policies? We got an email about it, and it seemed important."

"Evacuate?" Aggie repeated. "Why would we need to evacuate?"

"Just in case," her papa said. "Don't worry about it. It'll probably be super boring. I'm only going in case they have doughnuts." He squeezed Aggie, then let her sit up. "Do you have homework?"

"Of course I do," Aggie replied. "But I already did it."

Her papa grinned. "That's my girl."

✿✿✿

Jac came back from the surprise lemonade extravaganza slightly sweaty and sunburned, but with a big grin on her face. "We made so much money," she said. "Well, Adri did. I mostly just poured."

"Awesome," Aggie said from her bed. "That was nice of you to help."

"Did you know that she donates all the money from her sales to the children's hospital?" Jac said, flopping down on the floor next to Aggie, and when Aggie didn't respond, Jac sat up a little, her eyes just clearing Aggie's mattress. "What's up with you?"

"Nothing. I'm fine," Aggie said.

"Ha." Jac pushed herself up on her elbows. "You have five seconds to tell me or I'm going to tickle you."

Aggie smiled at that, mostly because she knew it wasn't a threat and Jac would very much do that to her. She had learned that lesson the hard way.

"It's just, Taylor transitioned last year and people were really mean to her. Not kids, but grown-ups. That's why she can't play on her old Little League team anymore."

Jac thought for a minute, her brow creasing as she turned that information over in her head. "Well, that's stupid," she said. "Who would get rid of Taylor? She's, like, the best pitcher ever! What, does her old team enjoy losing?"

"And she's really nice, too!" Aggie added, smacking her bed for emphasis. "Why are people so stupid sometimes?" Out of earshot of her dads, that word felt safe to use.

"Well, their loss," Jac said. "Because now we have a new friend and a great pitcher."

"And if anyone else is mean to her—"

"We'll kick them in the shins," Jac finished her sister's sentence.

That part, Aggie knew was only a threat. But still, it made her feel better.

"Yeah," she said. "Both shins."

Jac lay back down and held up her pinkie, and Aggie wrapped her own pinkie around Jac's, squeezing hard before letting go. "Hey," Jac said after a minute. "Marnie wants us to go to her piano recital."

"Cool."

"No, I mean like all of us. Dads, too. She said that this is her first recital after her parents split up, so she wants a lot of people there so that they don't make a scene."

Aggie sighed. *"Parents."*

From the floor, Jac nodded her agreement.

CHAPTER 10

JAC

"I? Am going to barf."

Jac had never seen Marnie look like that before. Usually at practice, she looked like she was about to take a cake out of the oven or become a contestant on one of those baking shows that Aggie loved, but now in the parking lot of some random community center, Marnie was pale and shaky-looking.

"You are not going to barf," Jac said, moving to grab her hands for some reassurance, but Marnie yanked her hands back, giving her an alarmed look. "Right, right, hands. Sorry."

"You are going to be fine," Tink said. She was wearing sparkly pink jeans and a sweatshirt that said "Sorry You're Not Me" in bright purple letters, and she had red plastic sunglasses over her eyes. Behind her, Josephine was wearing a huge, poofy pink dress and, Jac thought, looked like she was going to prom.

But to be honest, Josephine was not the one of Tink's siblings that Jac was hoping to see that afternoon.

"Did you know that there's a species of penguin called macaroni?" Josephine said to Marnie, then started to giggle. "Isn't that so funny? Do you still feel like barfing?"

Tink sighed and pushed her sister behind her. "Ignore her. You'll be fine."

"Who's going to be fine?" Aggie said. "I just saved us seats in the second row. Dads wanted the first row." She and Jac rolled her eyes at the mere thought of that. Jac would rather eat a live worm than sit in the front row of anything.

"Marnie's going to hurl," Josephine said, poking her head through Tink's folded arms. "It's gonna be awesome."

"Josephine, can you just go find Mom or Finn or something?"

Jac suddenly felt like she had shocked herself. "Finn's here?" she said, hoping that her voice didn't sound as strangled as it felt.

"Yeah, Mom made him come because we had to pick him up from his study group at the library and we didn't have time to go back home, so he just had to *deal* with it." Tink looked mostly annoyed by this development, which was definitely not how Jac felt.

"Marnie," Aggie said now. She was wearing her plastic jelly shoes, and Jac had helped her put her hair into a French braid. (Not without a lot of complaining on Aggie's part that Jac was pulling too tight. The things she did for her sister, Jac thought. She deserved a medal.)

"You're going to be fine," Aggie continued. "I watched you practice this song at least forty-five times on base last week."

Marnie nodded, gripping her elbows and hugging herself in the middle. "I'm not worried about the song!" she said. "I'm worried about *them*! Why did I invite so many people?" she said.

"Because your parents are both going to be here and you need moral support," Tink said. She was at least a head shorter than the rest of them, but there was a fiery look in her eyes. "And we're going to cheer and clap and yell for you and then it'll be done."

"WOOOOOOO!" Josephine cried, and Tink gave her a shove toward their mom, who was talking to Adriana's mom in the parking lot.

"Why is Josephine screaming?" Adriana said as she ran up. "Why aren't you inside?"

"Marnie's going to hurl," Aggie said.

"No, she's not," everyone else replied.

"Do you want some—" Adriana started to say.

"Do *not* offer me any lemonade right now," Marnie said, glaring at her friend.

"Well, fine," Adriana huffed, but she wisely didn't take the conversation any further.

"We can totally distract your parents if you need us to," Jac said.

"Josephine is the *perfect* distraction," Tink pointed out.

"WOOOOOO!!!"

"What's going on?" Taylor said. She had a boat-neck-style shirt on and dark jeans, but her sneakers were neon green. Jac could definitely appreciate a pop of color. "Why are you all— Whoa, Marnie, you look awful."

Everyone shot Taylor a look. "Sorry. What's going on?"

"Look, why don't you take her inside?" Jac said to Taylor and Adriana, who were both holding on to Marnie's arms. "That way she can get ready." And, she thought to herself, they'll be near a toilet just in case.

"Got it," Adriana said. "I saw both your mom and dad inside, and you'll be happy to know that they're sitting very far apart and they both seemed fine."

"I can't tell if that's good or bad," Marnie said shakily.

"Go," Jac mouthed to them.

"Would anyone even notice if she did forget?" Aggie whispered. "All piano songs kind of sound the same to me."

"It's not the recital," Tink said. "Her mom and dad separated last month, and this is, like, the first big thing they're doing together. Marnie's kind of a mess."

"Yeah, no kidding," Jac said.

"I thought Dylan's parents split," Aggie said, frowning a little.

"No, they divorced," Tink clarified. "Like, dunzo. Finito. No more."

"The ratings bonanza," Jac added, and Tink nodded.

"You practically need a spreadsheet to track whose parents are married and whose aren't," Aggie said with a sigh.

"I can make that happen," Adriana said.

"I was *kidding*," Aggie said. "Kind of."

"Girls!"

They all looked up to see Aggie and Jac's dads coming up to them. "That theater is filling up fast," their papa said. "C'mon, our programs are saving our seats, but we can't hold off the crowds for much longer."

"Did you know that there are *twenty-seven* kids performing at this?" their dad said, and didn't sound particularly thrilled about it. Their dads had been happy to go, happy to see Aggie and Jac making such good friends, happy to support them, but Jac suspected that they were having some second thoughts. "Twenty. Seven."

"Marnie's really talented," Aggie assured them. "So I'm sure the other kids are, too."

Tink caught her eye and shook her head a little.

"Oh," Aggie said. "Well, Marnie's talented enough to make up for the other twenty-six."

Jac saw both her parents wilt at that.

Their dads were just starting to herd everyone back inside when a bright white Tesla pulled up in the parking lot and the door opened like a spaceship and Dylan started to climb out. She was wearing a light blue denim miniskirt, a vintage NSYNC shirt, and a giant frown on her face. "It's fine," she was saying to the woman behind the wheel, who had a bouffant of long, cascading blond hair and giant sunglasses covering her eyes. "It's fine, Mom, forget about it."

Aggie and Jac immediately looked at one another, then at their dads.

Uh-oh.

"Oh. My. God." Their dad was covering his mouth. "Is that—"

"Do *not* make it weird," Jac whisper-hissed at them. "Dads. Pull it together."

"Are you friends with *Kelly Burton's daughter*?"

their other dad said. "And you didn't tell us?!"

"No!" Aggie hissed. "We knew you would make it weird!" They were sounding like a family of snakes at this point.

"We will be cool," their papa said, sounding very much like he would *not* be cool at all. "Do you think she needs a florist?"

"I totally forgot that they moved out to the canyon after the divorce," their dad said. Dylan was still standing by the passenger side of the car, arguing with her mom.

"Do not bring that up around Dylan!" Jac said.

"Ratings bonanza," Aggie and Tink whispered at the same time.

"Okay, okay, we're fine, we're cool, let's go inside." Their dad gave Jac a gentle shove toward Dylan. "Go get your friend, okay? She can sit with us. And if you make friends with any more kids of reality-TV celebrities, you are required to tell us *immediately*, okay?"

"Our family is so weird," Aggie said as Jac gave both their dads a final threatening look to keep it together before going over to Dylan, who was just starting to shut the car door.

"Hi," Jac said gently. "Is . . . ? Are you okay?"

"Fine," Dylan said. "Where's Marnie?"

"Adriana and Taylor took her inside," Jac said. "She's a little nervous."

"Has she threatened to puke yet?"

"Dylan, call me when you're done and I'll pick you up, okay?" Her mom called from the driver's seat. "Okay? Are you listening?"

"Yes, *Mother*," Dylan said, which made teeny tiny frown lines pop up on her mom's forehead before she slammed the car door shut. Jac was pretty sure that same behavior would have gotten her grounded for the rest of the year, but she didn't say anything.

"Marnie always gets nervous," Dylan said.

"Oh, okay," Jac said. She sort of felt out of her depth and suddenly wished Aggie had been the one sent to go fetch Dylan. Aggie was more sympathetic, more patient, or at least that's what Jac always thought.

"Are you sure you're . . . ?" Jac gestured toward the Tesla that was driving off.

"She said she'd come see Marnie, but she has to go film out in Calabasas," Dylan said. "I told her that we were all coming to support Marnie, but . . ." Dylan trailed off with a sigh. "It's fine. It's hot out here."

It was hot, the air so dry and breezy that it made Jac's eyes feel itchy. "Let's go inside," she said. "My dads saved us a bunch of seats."

Jac wouldn't often admit to this, but her dads had been right: Twenty-seven pianists was a LOT.

It had been interesting at first, but by number

eight, Jac was starting to think that maybe she would never want to hear the piano again. As each kid performed, a little pod of phones would pop up, the families gathered together to smile and film and murmur to themselves about how talented their kid was.

In between numbers seventeen and eighteen, Jac was pretty sure the lower half of her body was permanently numb, and she had to nudge her dad twice to make sure he didn't fall asleep when Taylor came out from the backstage area, her eyes searching for her friends. Jac happened to be on the aisle, so Taylor made a beeline for her.

"Jac," she whispered. "Can you come help me? Adri's mom called so she had to step outside and Marnie's still sort of freaking out."

Jac glanced at her dad, who just nodded and waved her off, so she snuck out of the room behind Taylor. "Are they playing tag?" Josephine said, and was quickly hushed by Tink and her mom.

Marnie was standing backstage by a folding table covered in snacks and juice boxes and bottled water, looking more like she was about to bungee jump into a ravine than play a four-minute piano piece. "Hi," she said shakily.

"I went and got reinforcements," Taylor told her, her face concerned. "Are you okay?"

"You really should have gotten Aggie or Tink," Jac said. "Seriously."

"No, you're good," Marnie said, taking deep breaths through her nose and letting them out through her mouth. "You're very steady and calm."

Jac had to take a beat and absorb this information, which was news to her.

"It's just, like, my mom's out there and my dad's out there, and *everyone* knows that they're not living together anymore, and that's all they're going to be thinking about. . . ." Marnie trailed off, and Jac was certain she saw a tiny bit of a lip tremble.

"You cannot cry," Jac said. "If you cry, I'll start to cry. I will not be steady and calm at all. Taylor will have to calm both of us down."

Marnie laughed a little at that, pressing the back of her wrists against her eyes. She had really long fingers and short fingernails that were painted a delicate seashell pink. Jac could see why she had taken up the piano.

"Who cares if they're thinking about your mom and dad?" Taylor said, patting her back. "Adults are always thinking about what the other adults are doing. It's like they don't have lives of their own."

"And if it helps, my dads have absolutely no idea about your parents," Jac added. "So at least two adults are completely oblivious." She paused. "What song are you playing?"

"It's an oldie. 'Girls Just Wanna Have Fun.'"

"My dad freaking loves that song," Jac said. "He'll probably start the wave or something and distract everyone. In fact, I bet I could ask both of them to do that if you want. They love a group activity."

Marnie laughed for real this time. "No, it's okay." She took another deep breath and wiped her eyes again. "I'm being ridiculous."

"It's not ridiculous," Taylor said. "You're nervous. It happens."

"And I haven't spent the past month watching you play baseball while wearing *oven mitts* just for you to back out now," Jac said, a mock scowl on her face. "So get out there and crush it."

Taylor smiled at Jac. "I'm glad you were the one on the aisle," she said. "I'm really bad with tough-love stuff."

"Okay," Marnie said for the last time, taking one more deep breath. "I'm ready. Let's do it."

When Jac and Taylor snuck back to their seats, Jac's dad scooted over to make room for them, then put his arm around Jac's shoulders. "Is your friend okay?" he whispered.

"Kind of," she replied. "If I ask you and Papa to start the wave, could you do it, though?"

"Absolutely," he said, then gave her a squeeze.

Marnie looked a smidge less pale when she finally came out on stage, clutching her sheet music and bowing a tiny bit at the applause. At opposite corners of the room, a woman and a man stood up, both of them grinning wildly and holding up their phones. Marnie's parents, Jac guessed. The man had Marnie's broad smile, and the woman, Marnie's midnight-black hair, although hers was shoulder-length and parted to the side.

"We now have Marnie Matson performing 'Girls Just Wanna Have Fun'—"

"Yesssss," Aggie and Jac's dad said under his breath. Aggie gave him a quick nudge.

"Marnie is twelve years old and, in addition to playing the piano, enjoys playing baseball with her friends." The piano teacher smiled indulgently as the girls all cheered. "That's me!" Josephine said proudly, and was once again shushed by everyone around her.

Marnie took such a deep breath that all of her friends could see it from the audience, and then she started to play. Her hands were shaking as they pressed down on the keys, and it sounded just fine to Jac, who had never even touched a piano in her entire life.

But then Marnie winced, a frown creasing her forehead, and winced again. She kept playing, and honestly, Jac hadn't even heard a wrong note, but clearly Marnie had, and when she was done and stood to take a bow, Jac could see the tears in her eyes.

The audience was applauding, though, with both of her parents giving her a standing ovation in their opposite corners of the auditorium. "Yeah, Marnie!" her dad yelled, giving her a thumbs-up, and Marnie smiled a very wobbly smile.

"That was great!" Jac's dad whispered once the applause died down and another kid came out to perform. "How many more are left?"

Jac glanced through the program. "Guess."

Her dad sighed. "Oh God."

When it was finally over, everyone gathered outside to congratulate all the performers. "That was so great!" Tink said as soon as Marnie came over to them. "You sounded amazing! I think it's the oven mitts. They gave you good luck."

"I messed up twice," Marnie said quietly. "Everyone heard."

"Yeah, but you didn't mess up a whole bunch of other times," Josephine said, beaming at her.

"And nobody even noticed," Taylor added, adjusting her headband behind her ears. "You're just a perfectionist, that's all."

"I've never messed up before!" Marnie said. "The nerves got to me."

"You know what?" Tink said. "I think we should have an after-party at my house."

"I really do not want to practice right now." Marnie sighed.

"No, not a practice. We can just hang out in the backyard."

"That sounds great," Adriana said, her voice deliberately sharp and bright. "Let's do it."

"A party!" Josephine said, clapping her hands together.

When Aggie and Jac finally climbed into their car, their dads were already in the front seats, their papa turning off the radio and their dad trying desperately to open a bottle of aspirin. "These aren't childproof—they're adult-proof," he muttered.

"Can we go over to Tink's when we get home?" Aggie asked, clicking her seat belt into place. "She wants to have an after-party for Marnie."

"Of course," her dad said, looking relieved as he managed to pry the lid off. "Tell your friend that she was really great. Very impressive." He passed the bottle to their papa, who took it without saying a word.

"She thinks she messed up twice," Jac said. "I didn't hear it, but she's all bummed out now."

"Aw, poor kid," their dad said as he started the car. "That's a lot of pressure."

"And her parents were there but they just separated, so it was weird," Aggie added.

"That's even more pressure. C'mon, dude, just

move already," their dad muttered to the car in front of them. "God, I need some caffeine."

As soon as they got home, Aggie and Jac scampered off to Tink's house, all too aware of how cranky their dads could get when they were caffeine deprived and not wishing to experience that any time soon. Jac, however, made a quick pit stop upstairs so she could brush her hair, change her shirt, and reapply her lip gloss. "Jac!" Aggie yelled up to her. "Come on!"

"It's not like we're going to be late or anything," Jac said as she thundered back down the stairs.

"Girls, please, indoor voices," their dad said. He was clutching a can of Diet Coke like a thirsty man in a desert.

"Well, we're going outside anyway," Jac said. "Bye!"

Her dad winced as she slammed the door behind them.

"Why are you so dressed up again?" Aggie asked, eyeing Jac suspiciously. "Are you wearing makeup?"

"I'm wearing lip gloss, and I just have an overall rosy glow," Jac said.

"And why did you change your shirt?"

"Because I felt like it!" Jac said, but she could feel the blush creeping up her cheeks and into her ears. Why did she care if Aggie knew she liked Finn? Why didn't she want to tell her?

Over at Tink's, the mood was anything but party-like.

"Everyone heard!" Marnie wailed. "And then both my mom and dad brought me flowers"—she gestured to the two bunches of sunflowers and purple irises next to her—"so then everyone was staring at me afterward!"

"I don't think *everyone* was staring at you," Taylor said. "Lots of kids got flowers."

Marnie continued on. "And they all saw my mom and dad sitting apart, so now it's like everyone knows that they're officially splitting up."

"People knowing is the worst," Dylan said quietly, and Taylor patted her hand.

"Sorry, Dyl," Marnie said, sniffling a little. "I know you have it a lot worse than me."

Dylan shrugged. "It's not a competition. And anyway, it still sucks."

"At least you didn't start over," Aggie said. "I don't think anyone even knew that you messed up. You kept going, right?" Jac knew this line of conversation all too well. Their dads were super into perseverance. She had heard the tune "Just keep swimming!" at least a million times in her life so far.

Marnie sniffled again. "I guess. It was just a long day. And usually after a recital, my mom and dad and I would go out to eat, but now I'm going out to dinner with my dad tonight and brunch with my mom tomorrow instead."

All the girls sighed at that, and Jac was grateful that nobody made a "At least you get two meals!" comment. Her dads were still married, of course, but she had known plenty of kids whose parents were divorced, and none of them were ever comforted by the "Hey, two birthdays! Two Christmases! Two Hanukkahs!" line of thought. She glanced over at Dylan, who was still looking down, her hair hiding her face.

"I'm just glad we have each other," Marnie said after a minute, her voice sounding both sad and fond. "You know? Sometimes it feels like friendship lasts longer than people's marriages."

"It's all Tink's fault," Taylor said, but she was smiling. "She's the one who makes us practice all the time."

"Yeah, what's that about?" Dylan said. "We never even play actual games." They could all tell she was teasing, though, especially when she wrapped an arm around Tink's narrow shoulders. "Why are we practicing all the time?"

Tink smiled and blushed, looking almost embarrassed for the first time since Jac had known her. "I don't know," she said. "It's just, like . . ." She trailed off before saying, "Sometimes it's nice to have somewhere to be with people you like."

The back screen door slammed open then and Josephine came crashing through the door holding a yellow box of Popsicles. She clearly had taken the "party" part of "after-party" seriously and was now wearing a blue-and-silver dress that looked like it came out of a box of dress-up clothes, and pink plastic shoes that had fake jewels and a tiny heel on them. A tiara was perched precariously on top of her head.

Josephine clearly subscribed to the "more is more" level of style, Jac thought. It was admirable.

"Here," Josephine said, thrusting the box at Marnie. "You had a bad day, so you get first pick." Then she paused before adding, "Just don't take the grape-flavored ones because those are my favorite."

"Josephine," Tink said, shaking her head.

"Fine."

Fortunately, Marnie grabbed a cherry-flavored Popsicle instead, and then Josephine passed the box to everyone else, saving her sister for last. "We serve the guests first," she said to Tink, who looked both amused and annoyed at the same time.

For a few minutes, there was no noise except for the slurping sounds of Popsicle eating and the sound of the wind chimes that someone (Jac guessed it was Tink and Josephine's grandma) had attached to the porch. "It's really hot," Aggie finally said, pulling her shirt away from her and fanning it a little. "It's hard to believe it's October."

"My grandma says that this is fire weather," Tink said. "But she's been saying that for fifteen years and nothing's ever happened, so . . ." She shrugged. "One year our toilet flooded because *someone* put their Barbie in it, though, but that's not the same."

"I *said* I was sorry," Josephine muttered.

The screen door slammed open again. "Where are the Popsicles?" a voice said, and Finn suddenly appeared on the porch. Jac immediately wanted to both hide and scramble to her feet at the same time.

"Here," Tink said, passing him the box, and he took it and went back inside. The whole experience took about five seconds, but Jac felt like she had been electrified.

And it was terrifying.

CHAPTER 11

AGGIE

Something was definitely up with Jac.

As Aggie helped clear the table that night (that was her chore, Jac's was taking out the trash every night, which Aggie personally thought was gross), she kept thinking about Jac's neatly brushed hair, her blushing face, the way she had turned her head to look at Finn when he came looking for the Popsicles that afternoon.

And Aggie didn't like how it made her feel.

So she decided to ignore it and move on to the other thought taking up way too much space in her brain.

"Dad," she said, passing him the now-empty lasagna pan so he could soak it. Aggie would eat lasagna every single night if she could. "Are you and Papa ever going to get divorced?"

Her dad looked at her with an expression that Aggie couldn't quite place. Something between love and sadness. "Is this because of your friend Marnie and her parents?"

"No," Aggie said immediately. Her dad raised an eyebrow at her. "Okay, maybe."

Her dad sighed and turned to face her, the dishes forgotten in the sink. "Listen to me," he said. "Sometimes parents split up and that's okay, but Papa and I still love each other very much and we're not splitting up. We not only love each other, but we *like* each other. Almost as much as we like you."

His mouth twitched into a smile at that, and Aggie smiled back, immediately comforted. She wasn't sure how they did it, but sometimes her dads seemed to know exactly what to say to make her feel better. "Well, I like you, too," she said.

"Excellent!" her dad replied, then planted a kiss on top of her head. "And because I like you so much, I'm going to let you scrub the lasagna pan tonight. No, no, don't thank me," he said, holding up a hand and backing out of the kitchen as Aggie started to protest. "I'm very happy to pass this privilege on to you."

"This is unfair!" Aggie yelled as soon as he disappeared. "This is unpaid labor, which is illegal!"

"Can't hear you!"

Aggie sighed, turned back to the casserole pan, and grabbed a sponge.

❂❂❂

Aggie saw Jac in the hallway a few days later at school, both of them on their way to lunch when she spotted a group of older girls walking toward her sister. All the eighth graders always seemed so huge, so tall. Aggie wasn't sure she could handle high school, what with all the juniors and seniors milling around and driving places. That seemed frighteningly adult, and Aggie shoved that thought to the back of her brain for now, something to dig out at three in the morning when she couldn't sleep and needed something to fret over.

"Hey," Aggie said, coming up next to Jac and then frowning when she saw the look in her twin's eyes. It wasn't fear, it wasn't annoyance, it was something Aggie had never seen there before.

Jac looked unsure.

"Oh, hiiiiii," one of the girls said. "You're a twin. Adorable."

Aggie could tell that she didn't think it was adorable at all, not with that tone in her voice. "No, clones," she said, mimicking the way Jac always sounded bored and annoyed when she said that, and one of the other girls huffed out a giggle before quickly steeling her expression again.

"Later, Jacaranda," the first girl said, walking just a little too close to Jac as they strolled away, and

Aggie watched until they turned the corner before she looked back at Jac.

"Who was that?" Aggie said, and felt almost relieved when she saw Jac's uncertain gaze fade back into its familiar annoyance.

"Nobody," Jac said, turning to open her locker. "Do you want to swap lunches?"

"Not really," Aggie said. "Are you friends with them or something?"

"So what if I am?" Jac said. "I'm allowed to make friends without you, you know."

"Duh," Aggie said, but she felt a bit like she had been stung by a mosquito, that first tiny itch growing into something more painful, more irritating by the minute. "They just kind of seemed like jerky friends is all."

"Don't worry about it," Jac said. "Okay?"

"I can't worry about you?" Aggie said. "Why aren't you telling me what's going on? About anything?" About Finn, she wanted to say, but she bit it back just in the nick of time. She wasn't even sure what she wanted to say about that, or why it made her so upset.

After school, Aggie and Jac walked in tense silence up to Tink's house, just in time to see her bounding down the steps of her house, Josephine (of course) in tow. "So!" Tink announced. "We can't practice here today because my grandma has a headache."

"Because of *me*," Josephine said, seeming almost proud of this dubious honor.

"Soooo," Tink said again, drawing a line on the ground with her toe before looking at the twins. "Do you think we could practice at your house today?"

"Sure." Aggie shrugged. "My dad is home but I don't think he'll care."

After a quick round of text messages to the rest of the girls, they decamped back to Aggie and Jac's house. "Daaaaad!" Jac yelled in through the front door. "We're practicing here today!"

"'Kay!" came back the response. "Watch the windows!"

Jac gave him a thumbs-up through the front door. "It's all good," she said. "I don't think any of us except Aggie can hit that far."

"I'll aim for the neighbors' house," Aggie called after Jac.

"Do *not* aim for the neighbors' house!" their dad yelled back. "Don't aim for *anyone's* house!"

"Roger that," Jac said.

Adriana and Taylor came wandering up a few minutes later, both of them wearing T-shirts that had a sketch of a bunch of lemons on them. "I got roped in," Taylor said, shooting Adriana a dirty look. "I think I squeezed fifty lemons today."

"Hi!" Marnie called as she strolled up, seeming like she was in a much better mood than she had been the last time everyone had seen her. She even had a brand-new pair of oven mitts tucked under her arm. They were very clean-looking and had an intricate fruit pattern swirled across them. Aggie wondered if she had a drawer in her dresser reserved solely for protective hand wear. "Cool, a new practice spot!"

She was about to add something else when a car swung into the twins' driveway and their papa hopped out of the driver's seat. "Hey!" he said. "What's the occasion?"

"I gave my grandma a headache," Josephine announced from their front lawn, where she was practicing her handstands.

"You don't say," their papa replied, looking bemused.

"Dad said it was okay for us to practice here today," Aggie said as Jac caught Josephine just before she tumbled to the ground.

"Yeah, of course," he said. "Let me know if you need any tips." He pretended to hit a ball out of the park, but Aggie wasn't buying it.

"When was the last time you even held a bat?" she asked him.

"I think 1989."

"Then we're good, thanks," she replied. "But that

is my favorite Taylor Swift album."

He planted a quick kiss to the top of her head before going inside. "Mine too. Let us know if you need snacks or anything, or if anyone's curious about how to diversify your stock portfolios in time for tax season!"

"Will do," Jac said as she set Josephine back on her feet.

Just as their papa disappeared inside, a familiar white Tesla pulled up to the curb and the driver's side window rolled down. "Hey, girls!" Kelly Burton called. "Wait 'til you see what Dylan got!"

Dylan climbed out of the passenger seat, looking both pleased and embarrassed through her curtain of long red hair. "Hey," she said to them.

"Here, I'll help you," Kelly said, then parked the car and started to help Dylan unload a huge duffel bag from the trunk.

Aggie turned back to look at her house and saw the curtain move slightly, two dad-like figures conveniently disappearing from view as soon as she glanced their way. She made a cut-throat motion at them, giving them a strong glare for good measure.

She was starting to think that maybe screen-time limits needed to be extended toward the adults in their house, rather than the kids.

"It's really heavy," Dylan said, dropping the bag

on the ground and unzipping it. "Josephine, can you please give me some space?"

Josephine, who had immediately zoomed over as soon as she saw the bag, backed up a quarter of an inch.

Meanwhile, Aggie couldn't help but notice that Dylan's mom was in full hair and makeup, with high heels and a nice dress. Was she going somewhere in the afternoon? Why was she so dressed up? Was this just what it was like to be famous? It seemed uncomfortable, especially in the heat of the mid-October day. Aggie was just wearing jean shorts and a shirt from Target and she was already starting to sweat under the afternoon sun.

"Look!" Dylan said, holding up a catcher's mask, and the rest of the girls and Kelly all gathered around as she started to unload a full catcher's uniform, complete with pads and a special mitt. "My mom got it for me." She beamed up at Kelly, who smiled back.

"Try it on!" Kelly said.

The girls all helped Dylan shuffle into the uniform, giggling as they tried to fit the pads onto her narrow shoulders and yanking the mask down over her face. "This is way better than oven mitts," Marnie said.

"Anything's better than oven mitts," Adriana teased her, giving her a nudge in the ribs when Marnie rolled her eyes.

"How do I look?" Dylan said, her voice muffled behind the mask.

"So professional!" Kelly said, holding up her phone to take a picture. Dylan seemed to wilt a tiny bit, but Aggie wasn't sure if it was just the weight of the equipment. "Smile!"

All the girls grinned automatically, but Kelly waved them away. "No, just Dilly, girls," she said, and Dylan sagged a little more.

"Mom," she started to say.

"Just one video," Kelly said. It almost sounded like their roles were reversed and Kelly was asking permission to stay up just thirty minutes later, *please, please, please.*

"Mom—"

"Girls, can I talk to Dylan for a second?" Kelly said, coming to her daughter's side and stroking her hair. "Just for a quick minute."

"Um, yeah, of course," Tink said, pulling Josephine away as the rest of them went back toward the house, very quietly and stealthily rearranging the beanbag bases and definitely not eavesdropping at all.

Nope, not even a little bit.

"Dilly," Kelly said, bending down a little to Dylan's height, and even from that distance, Aggie could see Dylan's shoulders bend in, like a little protective cage. "It's just one video. Thirty seconds at the most."

"Mom—"

"Baby, you know money's tight right now." Kelly reached up and started to stroke Dylan's hair again. Aggie could see the gleam of a diamond ring on the middle finger of her hand. "I'm trying to generate new streams of revenue because you know your dad and I . . ." A frown crossed Kelly's face, barely. "Well, when I told this company that you were the catcher for your girls' baseball team—"

"It's gender inclusive," Dylan muttered. "And we've never even played an actual game before."

"—they offered to send over all this gear in exchange for a sponsored post! Isn't that so great?"

It did not appear to sound great to Dylan, who was looking at the ground instead of at her mom. "Fine," she said quietly. "Just one video."

"That's my girl!" Kelly stood up to her full height, beaming. "Besides, I need everyone to see how cute my best daughter is." She chucked Dylan on the chin, then pulled out her phone. "C'mon, show me how you do it, you little superstar!"

By the time Kelly finally kissed Dylan goodbye and drove away, Dylan looked so sad that Aggie had to resist the urge to run over to her and give her a hug. The silence was awkward, so awkward that even Josephine was still and quiet.

"Okay!" Tink finally said, clapping her hands

together, and all the girls jumped simultaneously. "Let's start practicing. We still have time—"

It was then that Dylan ripped off her catcher's mask and burst into tears. Nobody moved at first, and as Dylan started to rip off the rest of her gear piece by piece, her tears grew louder.

Aggie couldn't take it anymore and ran over to her. "Dylan, it's okay!" she cried. "It's not a big deal—it's just a video!"

"It is so a big deal!" Dylan sobbed, struggling with her chest protector. "She posts the video and gets all the money, but then all these strangers comment and then all of her fan accounts post it again and then my dad gets mad and then they fight on the phone!"

Aggie patted her now-bare shoulder awkwardly, not sure what to say as the other girls started to crowd around them, dodging a knee pad as Dylan tossed it to the ground.

"It's not fair!" Dylan cried. "I don't want to be the catcher anymore! I'm done!"

It was then that Aggie and Jac's dad appeared in the doorway, wearing what they both called "the Dad look," his glasses askew on the top of his head. "What's wrong?" he called, coming down the front steps and hurrying down the path toward the girls. "Is someone hurt? Did you have a fight?"

"Dylan's mom made her do a sponsored video," Jac explained, now patting Dylan's back as she sniffled. "And she doesn't want to be the catcher anymore."

There were times when Aggie was absolutely mortified by their parents: when their dad put on old disco albums and danced around the living room, when their papa wore black socks, and that one time when they got lost in the car and didn't have cell service and they had to pull over to ask someone for directions. Aggie had wished she could evaporate into space after that experience, she was so embarrassed. But then there were times like these when she wouldn't have traded her dads for any other parents in the world.

"Well, we can't have that," her dad said, putting his arm around Jac's shoulders. "Dylan's the best catcher you have. Why don't you all come inside and have a snack and maybe we can sort it out, hmm?"

"Snacks?" Josephine said, perking up. "Are they vegan?"

Everyone looked at her, even Dylan. "Are *you* vegan?" Tink asked in disbelief.

"No." Josephine shrugged. "It just seemed polite to ask."

Dylan was the first to giggle, wiping at her eyes. "Josephine," she said. "You are truly something else."

Josephine beamed. "Thank you."

Once inside, the girls all gathered around their farmhouse dining room table (which their parents had gotten for an absolute steal on Facebook Marketplace, blah blah blah, Aggie and Jac never wanted to hear that story again), with Dylan at the center of their group. Taylor ran outside to pick up all of Dylan's abandoned catcher's gear, shoving it into the duffel bag and dragging it back inside the house. "This is heavy," she panted. "Are you really supposed to wear that and play at the same time?"

"No," Dylan said. "Because I'm never playing again!"

"You have to play," Tink said, looking a little desperate. "You heard Aggie and Jac's dad—you're our best catcher ever. You can actually catch the ball!"

"Hey," Marnie said, looking a little offended. "I can catch and I'm wearing *oven mitts*."

"Fine," Tink said. "Everyone's a great catcher. But, Dylan, you're the *best*. That's probably why your mom wants to post a video of you, because you're so great!"

It was extremely clear to everyone at the table that Dylan was not buying what Tink was selling.

Their dad came back in then with a tray of cut-up fruit and a pile of those little cheeses that were wrapped in red wax. Josephine immediately reached for one, but Adriana took it out of her hands and unwrapped it for her before Josephine could eat the wax. "That's the last thing we need," Adriana muttered before passing the cheese back to Josephine.

"Thanks, Dad," Aggie said as Jac gave him a one-armed hug around his waist. Aggie was of the firm belief that if someone took the time to cut up fruit for you and your friends, that meant they really loved you a whole lot.

"And I haven't even seen my dad in almost a month," Dylan continued. "Only on his Instagram page. He met some new girlfriend, and they went to Hawaii to escape the cameras, at least that's what he said. But they're still posting a bunch of photos all the time." She sniffled again, and Aggie felt her heart break. She couldn't imagine not seeing her dads for a month, not even when she was an adult. Yes, they were embarrassing and annoying and sometimes got grouchy and nagged a whole bunch, but they were her dads. They and Jac and Aggie were a package deal.

"Dylan," Marnie said gently. "I know it's not my business, but have you talked to your mom about any of this?"

"No," Dylan said. "She's really busy and stressed out. I don't want her to be even more stressed out because of me. I heard her on the phone the other day—she was saying that she wasn't sure she could make the house payments anymore, but my dad said that she was just saying that and they got into another fight."

"Maybe you *should* tell your mom these things," Taylor said. "She might be stressed out and everything, but you're still her kid."

Josephine stealthily reached out for another cheese wedge before Tink took it out of her hand and replaced it with grapes. She pouted but ate them anyway.

"She even—" Dylan started to say, choking up again, then looked up at their dad before looking away.

"Dad, I think we need drinks," Jac said. It was a very obvious ploy to get their dad out of the room, which he thankfully understood.

"Eight La Croixs coming up!" he said, disappearing back into the kitchen with a speed that surprised Aggie.

"She even wanted the producers to do a show when I got my first period!" Dylan said.

"Nooooooo," said every single girl in the room, even Josephine.

"I know, right?" Dylan said. "She said it'd be useful for other people who were also starting their periods, that they'd have someone to 'look up to' or whatever, but I said no way."

Aggie was starting to feel very warm, and she and Jac exchanged a quick glance across the table before looking away.

Because the truth was that neither of them had started their periods yet.

Aggie knew Jac would be the one to get it first, though.

It wasn't like they didn't know it was coming. Their dads had had the discussion with them, of course, completely with diagrams (barf) and even a few YouTube videos (ugh). There were baskets in every single bathroom in their house with pads and tampons and supplies, ready and waiting for whoever needed them. "This is the weirdest gift basket I've ever gotten," Jac had deadpanned when their dads had presented them to the girls. "Thanks, I think?"

Aggie tried hard not to think about what it would be like for Jac to get it first. And it wasn't even that she was jealous, because she *wasn't*. She knew periods were a fact of life, that lots of people had them, that it was nothing to be scared of, whatever. But it felt very strange that Jac could experience something that Aggie hadn't, that Jac could have this brand-new life and Aggie would be somehow behind her, and there was nothing she could do to catch up with her sister.

And based on things she had heard from other girls in the school bathroom, Aggie wasn't sure she even wanted to start her period! Aggie found herself both desperate to start and terrified of the moment when she did. Would she be home? In bed? *At school???* There were too many open-ended questions, and Aggie was definitely not a fan of those. She liked to know what was going to happen, especially with her own *body* for goodness' sake.

"That's totally inappropriate!" Adriana said now at Dylan's admission. "You shouldn't have your private life all over the place."

"She apologized later," Dylan said. "But you know. Still." She wiped at her eyes. "I just don't want to feel like I'm only good for ratings, you know?"

Their dad reappeared then with an armful of flavored seltzer cans, setting them down on the dining room table. Aggie wondered how much he had heard. "Dylan, you're welcome to stay as long as you'd like," he said.

"Can she stay for dinner?" Aggie asked.

"Sure, of course," her dad said.

Dylan nodded glumly and reached for her phone, her thumbs tapping out a quick message. It only took a minute before the reply zoomed back, and all of them—even the girls' dad—leaned forward a little, as if they could somehow see the response.

"My mom says she's going to come pick me up," Dylan said. "She wants to talk."

"Well, that's great!" their dad said. "Communication is so important between parents and kids. I remember—"

"Dad." Aggie caught his eye and shook her head. Now was definitely not the time for a Parental Life Lesson.

"Right," he said. "Well, I'll just be upstairs if you need anything."

"Great!" Jac said, standing up as if to usher him away. "Thanks for the snacks and drinks. We're good now, all fed and hydrated." She patted his back as he walked away.

"Your dads are really nice," Dylan sniffled as soon as he was out of the room, and it was just the girls again. "Seriously. You're so lucky."

Aggie and Jac exchanged another furtive glance, this one much less loaded than the last. They knew how lucky they were to have their dads, no matter how embarrassing they sometimes became. "Well, they're lucky to have *us*," Jac said brightly. "Aggie and I are practically perfect!"

That broke the tension, and Dylan smiled for the first time since she had shown up at practice. "Well, I wouldn't go *that* far," she said, then squealed and laughed as she dodged a flying cheese wedge.

When Kelly finally pulled up at the curb in her white Tesla, eight pairs of eyes were watching from the front window. (Well, ten pairs, if the girls had known about their dads watching from the office upstairs.) "Do you want us to come out with you?" Taylor asked.

"Down, girl," Dylan said to her, but then put her arm around Taylor's shoulders and gave her a squeeze. "No, I'm fine. I just need to talk to my mom. Like, *really* talk."

"Boundaries," Adriana said with a nod. "They're very important. At least that's what my mom says. She's a therapist," she added to Aggie and Jac. "Let me know if you need her card."

Aggie and Jac both shook their heads as Kelly opened her car door. She still had her big sunglasses on, but even from behind those, Aggie could tell that she looked upset, almost like she had been crying. "Her hair is soooo pretty," Josephine said from around a mouthful of cheese. (She had managed to sneak another one without her sister catching her.)

"It's a wig," Dylan replied. "She has a whole bunch of them."

"Gorgeous." Josephine sighed.

"Okay, here I go," Dylan said.

"Break a leg," Aggie told her. One of her dad's friends back in San Francisco had performed most weekends in a drag queen brunch and had told her that it was bad luck to wish a performer good luck; you were supposed to say "break a leg" instead, which to Aggie seemed ridiculous, but okay.

"That's mean," Josephine muttered as she gave Aggie a dirty look.

They all watched as Dylan trudged outside, dragging the dreaded duffel bag behind her. Kelly got out of the car, pushing her sunglasses up into her (fake) hair, and when Dylan was close enough, she reached out her arms and enveloped her in a hug.

"Oh, that's sweet," Adriana said.

"Is she crying?" Marnie added, pressing her nose against the window.

"She might be," Taylor replied. "But allergies are really awful right now with all the Santa Ana winds. She could just have itchy eyes."

"Aww, she's still hugging her!" Aggie said. "That's a good sign."

"Or she could be half boa constrictor," Jac replied, then giggled as she got a flurry of shoulder punches from her friends.

"Way to kill the mood," Taylor said.

"Girls?" their dad said, and the seven of them slowly turned around, looking guilty. "Let's maybe let Dylan and her mom have some privacy, what do you think?"

"I mean, she'll probably talk about it on the show, so—" Tink started to say, but their dad raised an eyebrow. "I mean, yes, privacy is very important."

"If you want to practice, you can use the backyard," he said. "Just watch out for the windows. You kids have *no* idea how expensive windows are."

The last thing any of them wanted was to get into a boring grown-up conversation about how life was sooooo hard when you were an adult, like being a preteen girl was all rainbows and sunbeams and unicorns named Prancer. "Got it," Jac said, starting to herd everyone else outside. "Windows. Terrible. Avoid. Noted."

Even though practice went fine and no windows were shattered, Aggie felt agitated for the rest of the evening. She couldn't put her finger on why, but it was like her skin felt hot and tight, even after she checked twice in the bathroom mirror to make sure she wasn't sunburned.

That night at dinner, their dad set down his fork and reached for his water glass. "So," he said, "big day coming up."

Aggie and Jac both rolled their eyes simultaneously. "Daaaad," Jac said. "Thirteen is not that big of a big deal."

"It's a huge deal!" their papa protested. "You're going to be teenagers!"

"*Sixteen* is a big deal," Jac said. "Not thirteen. Thirteen is like a nothingburger year now."

Aggie nodded in solidarity, pushing her black beans around on her plate. "It's like turning twenty-nine instead of thirty."

Their dads managed to hide their amused smirks. "Got it," their dad said. "Okay, so even though it's a 'nothingburger year'—which, where did you even learn that phrase—"

"YouTube."

"Of course. Anyway, a birthday is still a birthday, which means a celebration, which means we need to figure out your birthday activity this year!"

It was a hard and fast rule in their family that they no longer did birthday parties, not after the Great Deflating Bounce House Incident at their fourth birthday party. That was fine with the girls because instead of a party, they got dinner at the restaurant of their choice and a shopping trip to their favorite store. Aggie and Jac knew this routine by heart, and it was one that Aggie hoped would never change.

"So where are we going this year?" their dad asked.

"When do we get to go to Hawaii like you did for your birthday last year?" Jac asked.

"When you get a job and turn forty," he replied. "Continental US only. Preferably within a twenty-mile radius of our house."

Aggie grinned to herself. "Build-A-Bear and Cheesecake Factory!" she cried just as Jac said "Sephora and Katsuya!"

Aggie felt like she had been slapped in the face. Jac *always* said Build-A-Bear and Cheesecake Factory. It was their tradition. Aggie loved going to pick out her stuffed bear, finding all the accessories, and coming up with the perfect name. (Jasper, Halo, and Nala upstairs would all attest to her excellent stuffed-animal naming skills.)

And Cheesecake Factory! Who doesn't want to eat at a restaurant named after dessert?! Aggie loved the high-backed booths, the huge mugs of refillable drinks, and the never-ending bread basket. Their menu was so big that it had *page numbers*!

What even *was* Katsuya? Did they even have cheesecake?

"What's Katsuya?" she asked, feeling crankier by the second.

"It's sushi," Jac said, looking excited. "They have crispy rice with spicy tuna. Adriana told me all about it. It sounds awesome. And this one YouTuber I follow did a whole video about Sephora and her favorite skin care buys and sheet masks and—"

"Sounds stupid," Aggie muttered. "Why would you even want your rice to be *crispy*?"

"Aggie." Her papa shot her a look. He had a rogue leaf stuck in his hair. Normally Aggie would think it was funny but now she just found it aggravating. "You and Jac can pick different birthday celebrations, you know that. Don't call it stupid."

"And it's not stupid!" Jac protested. "Just because

I don't want my twenty-fifth stuffed bear doesn't mean—"

"Who doesn't want a stuffed bear?" Aggie cried, then threw her napkin on the table and stood up abruptly.

"Aggs, we don't throw—"

"And Sephora is stupid, too!" Aggie said. Her chest was feeling hot and tight, her breath making her lungs hurt. She hadn't been this angry in so long. She hadn't felt this *betrayed* in so long. And the worst part was that she wasn't sure who she was even angry at to begin with. Was it Jac, picking these grown-up places in the first place? Or (and Aggie only entertained this thought for a second before shoving it back down in her brain) was Aggie mad at herself for not picking them, too, like she should have known better, been more grown up?"

"Who cares about stup—"

"Agapanthus."

"—dumb makeup and whatever else you're supposed to buy there? It's just a waste of time."

"Aggie!" her papa said sharply, even as Jac's face was quickly becoming a thundercloud.

"Forget it," Aggie said. "Go do your birthday by yourself, I don't care. Maybe you should take Adriana with you since it was all her idea? And crispy rice sounds stale, not even *good*."

And then she turned and ran up the stairs, ignoring the sounds of her dads calling her back.

She stayed up on her bed for a long time, watching the sun set and the orange streetlights come on. She carefully tucked Jasper, Nala, and Halo around her, feeling a little silly and a little lonely at the same time. She had too much pride to go back downstairs and apologize for her outburst, and besides, she wasn't sure she was even that sorry.

Sometimes being angry was easier than being sad.

She heard the rest of her family get ready for bed, and she half expected her dads to come in and tell her to change into pajamas or brush her teeth or that she was grounded or whatever, but as the sky went from purple to black, nobody knocked on her door. She heard Jac say good night to their dads, heard the sounds of water running and locks turning, securing the house for the night. She could even hear Jack the Rat running on his wheel in the living room before their dad threw a towel over the cage.

Aggie fell asleep in her clothes, her cheek pressed into her pillow, surrounded by her animals, exhausted by her own self.

She woke up the next morning to an earthquake.

At least, that's what she thought it was at first. Something was shaking her gently, and by the time

Aggie was able to open her eyes, she realized that it wasn't an earthquake shaking her; it was her dad.

"Aggs," he whispered. "C'mon. I've got to make a delivery to the hotel this morning. Wanna come with me?"

Aggie blinked and tried to focus. She had been having a dream where she was flying a plane filled with ducks and they were all going to Hawaii, and the ducks were getting restless. Maybe it had been more of a nightmare than a dream. "Time is it?" she asked, rubbing at her eyes.

"Almost seven," her dad said. "Your dad and Jac are still sleeping."

Aggie stretched, tilting her head backward so she could look out of her window. "'Kay," she mumbled. "Ten minutes?"

"Eight," her dad replied, then gave her hip a pat before standing up to his full height. "Meet you in the car."

Eight and a half minutes later, Aggie was sliding into the passenger seat of her dad's delivery van, wearing her favorite pink Hello Kitty hoodie (the hood had tiny ears and the iconic bow) that she had snuck into Jac's room to find. It had been slung over Jac's desk chair, and Aggie made a mental note to remind Jac that other people's possessions deserved to be treated with respect, ahem.

That was, as soon as she was talking to Jac again.

The gloom of the previous night dissipated a bit as Aggie and her dad backed out of their driveway and started down the hill into Los Angeles. The sun's honey-colored rays were just starting to stretch over the canyon, twisting their way through the overgrown vines and trees that lined the streets, and for the first time since they had moved there, Aggie thought that maybe this new city finally felt like home.

They drove past a fire danger sign, the giant bear pointing to a meter that said "WARNING! VERY HIGH!" and Aggie's dad clicked his tongue in response. "That's not good," he said. "It's so dry and with these winds . . ." He left the rest of his thought unsaid, and Aggie felt a small flicker of flame blaze in her brain before she quickly put it out. The thought was too scary to imagine, especially when she had been awake for only ten minutes so far.

The city was quiet as her dad turned onto Sunset Boulevard. All the fancy hotels and restaurants and comedy clubs were empty, making the city feel like it was only open to locals, making Aggie feel a little more awake.

"I know what you're doing," she finally said as he turned off of Sunset and headed down the hill into the heart of the city.

"And what is it that I'm doing?" her dad replied, sounding amused.

"You're trying to get me to talk to you because it's easier to talk to kids in the car. That way, we don't have to look at each other."

Her dad glanced at her, then started to laugh. "And just exactly how do you know this?"

Aggie looked at him then, breaking the first rule of talking in the car. "I heard it on NPR," she said. "You and Dad shouldn't listen to smart radio stuff while Jac and I are around. We learn a lot of things."

Her dad grinned. "Busted," he said. "On all counts. Sooooo. Wanna talk?"

Aggie crossed her arms and looked out the window. The longer she was awake, the more she remembered of the night before, and the heavier her chest started to feel. It was like everything around her was so familiar, so comfortable, and she still felt displaced and homesick.

"It's just that everything's changing," she said quietly, and her dad reached forward and turned off the oldies '80s music that he had been playing. "It's changing too fast, and I don't like it."

"Like how?"

"Like . . ." Aggie played with her hoodie strings, pulling them so that the hood tightened around her face. "Like Jac is changing and I'm not."

Just saying it out loud made hot tears come to her eyes.

"Am I a total weirdo?" she asked.

"Oh, Aggs," her dad sighed, then pulled the van over and killed the engine, turning in his seat so he could face her.

"You're doing it wrong!" Aggie protested. "You're supposed to keep driving so we don't have to look at each other!" She swiped at her eyes, only for more tears to appear.

"I'll decide the rules," her dad said, not unkindly. "Say more."

"And like . . ." Aggie sighed. "She wants to eat sushi and she knows about things that I don't understand or even like, and I feel like I have to like those things, too, or . . . or she won't like me anymore."

Well, that was that. Aggie was full-on crying now.

"Agapanthus," her dad murmured, and that's how Aggie knew she was really upset, because she didn't even get mad at him for using her full name. "Jac would never not like you. She loves you. You're sisters. You're her twin. You've known each other for literally your entire lives."

"But that's exactly it!" Aggie cried. "I've known her for so long, and now it's like I don't know her at all. She wants to wear sheet masks, and I feel like everything I do is babyish and she's all sophisticated and mature or whatever." Aggie crossed her arms over her chest again, and sighed. "I guess I don't know how to keep up."

"Okay," her dad said. "Look at me. Seriously, look at me."

Aggie very reluctantly turned in her seat to face him, wishing she could pull her hoodie so tight that it would completely cover her face, a Hello Kitty costume with no room for a mouth.

She should have stayed in bed.

"You and Jac are growing up," he said quietly. "And that means that you're going to change. And however you go about doing that is perfectly fine, for both of you."

"Easy for you to say," Aggie muttered, using the cuff of her hoodie sleeve to wipe at her eyes. "It's not your twin sister who's totally being different than you."

"That is true," her dad said. "But you know that Papa and I love you both, regardless of how different you are and become."

Aggie did know that. But it was still good to hear that.

Her dad laughed. "You want to know something else that's true?"

Aggie nodded.

"Crispy rice with spicy tuna is delicious."

Aggie was unconvinced. "But Cheesecake Factory has cheesecake."

"And page numbers on their menus!" her dad said.

"Exactly!" Aggie sat up in her seat, drawing her knees up to her chest. "They have *Glamburgers*."

"We're going to have to agree to disagree on that one," her dad said. "But we can go to both. And we can do Build-A-Bear *and* Sephora. You and Jac have always done the same thing, and it's okay if things change. It just means new adventures. The important things will stay the same.

"*But*," he added, "you should probably apologize to Jac."

Aggie didn't respond, but she knew he was right. Fighting with her sister always made her feel like she had a pebble in her shoe that she couldn't shake out. She still felt kind of weird about everything, though. "I guess," she said. "But maybe later this afternoon. Jac's always kind of cranky in the morning."

"I know," her dad said as he started up the van again. "That's why I always wake you up to come with me instead."

Aggie preened a little at that. When you spent your whole life looking like someone else, it was good to feel unique every once in a while.

When they got to the hotel, Aggie carried in one of the smaller arrangements, hydrangeas and sunflowers and orange-colored roses tickling her chin, while the doorman held the door for her and her dad struggled with one of the bigger arrangements.

It always made her feel proud to see all of her dad's hard work displayed in some of the most beautiful hotels she had ever seen. This was the reason they had moved to Los Angeles, since her papa could do his job from anywhere, so long as he had a laptop and coffee. (And the coffee was more important than the laptop, he often said.) But she had spent a lot of her childhood wandering through flower markets, some of the plants towering over her head like the roses in *Alice in Wonderland*, and now to see her dad unloading display after display of gorgeous flowers, it made Aggie's heart grow ten times bigger.

On the way home up the canyon, her dad gestured to the Country Store on the side of the road. "Want to stop for a treat?" he said.

"Yes," Aggie replied before he could even finish his sentence.

There was a coffee cart just outside the store, and there was a long line of parents, kids, and dogs waiting for their coffee. Aggie chose a banana muffin and a steamed milk, then at the last minute picked out a blueberry muffin for Jac. "Apologies are easier with food," she said to her dad.

"Totally agree," he replied.

While they waited for her dad's (extremely complicated) coffee order, Aggie wandered around the front of the store to her favorite spot: a large mural of blue and yellow sunbeams and a red heart in the middle of them. There was a round mirror at the center of the heart, and the words "YOU ARE HERE" painted in big green bubble letters.

"Can I borrow your phone?" she asked her dad, who handed it over. She opened up the camera, then held her fingers in a peace sign, made a kissy face, and took a photo of herself.

She was here.

CHAPTER 12

JAC

The blueberry muffin *did* help Aggie's apology go down somewhat easier, Jac had to admit. She used her newly pink-painted fingernails to pluck out each blueberry as she sat across from Aggie at the kitchen table, watching her sister fidget her way through saying sorry.

"If you want to do separate things for our birthday, that's fine," Aggie said, poking at her own muffin. "I was just upset and cranky."

"Cool," Jac said. "You'll like Katsuya."

"How do you know? You've never even been."

"Because." Jac popped a blueberry into her mouth. "I can just tell."

Aggie looked dubious but didn't argue, which Jac felt was a win.

The rest of the day passed with little fanfare, with Aggie and Jac still doing the post-fight dance around each other. Aggie was overly polite to her and Jac was quiet, digging out in the garden with their papa and then watering their newly planted roses. Aggie disappeared over to Tink's house for a while and came back with her hair in skewed pigtails. "Josephine" was all she said.

"Yikes," Jac replied. "That's a look."

Aggie tried to use the side of the toaster to look at her hair. "It's worse than I thought. Can you help me take it out?"

Jac surveyed the situation. "I don't know. You might be beyond help."

"Jac!"

"I'm kidding, I'm kidding. But we might need to use Dad's gardening shears."

"Jac!"

"I'm kidding!"

In the end, they managed to work together to release Aggie's hair from the bevy of rubber bands, clips, and barrettes that Josephine had used. "What in the world?" their dad said as he came into the room.

Jac just held up one hand as she used the other to try to twist out a unicorn-shaped barrette. "Don't ask."

Their dad sighed. "Josephine?"

"Josephine." The girls sighed.

✲✲✲

Things got very exciting at their next practice.

Dylan was behind the plate, crouched down in the catcher's uniform that her mom's sponsors had gifted her. After all the drama of the sponsored post, she seemed calmer. "My mom and I talked a lot that night," she told her friends as she tugged on her gear. "And we agreed that we're not doing any more posts about me or my life. I'm off-limits unless *I* want to do something."

"That is awesome," Tink said. "Good for you for talking to your mom! I'm proud of you!"

Adriana stood behind her and made exaggerated cheerleader moves, which made everybody else laugh.

"Hey!" Tink said, but even she was laughing, too. "I'm a positive person. What can I say?"

They all went to their respective positions after that, with Aggie stepping up to the plate. She was wearing shorts that Jac was 99 percent sure belonged to her. Annoying.

"C'mon!" Josephine cried as Taylor started to wind up, watching Dylan for her signal. "Throw it into the dirt! We want a pitcher, not a belly itcher!"

Taylor stopped. "Josephine, you are the worst trash-talker ever!"

"C'mon, Taylor, strike her out!" Marnie yelled.

"You can do it!" Tink shouted, followed quickly by her cry of "Let's go, Aggie!"

Aggie, annoyingly enough, had a habit of hitting the ball way down the street, so far that their resident outfielder, Josephine, wasn't even allowed to go that far by herself. She never got a base hit, so Jac readied herself at first for another round of her sister's gloating as she lazily jogged around the bases.

Left field (also known as the neighbor's driveway) was suspiciously quiet, and Jac glanced over to see Josephine crouched by the grass, poring through a patch of clover. "Josephine!" Tink shouted. "Eyes on the game!"

"I need to find a four-leaf clover!" she yelled back without looking up.

"Doesn't matter. I'm going to hit it past her anyway!" Aggie said.

That got Josephine's attention. She looked up, stuck her tongue out, and then went back to her clover business.

Taylor started to wind up again, Aggie pulled the bat back, Dylan gave the signal, and Taylor sent the ball flying.

Aggie swung and missed.

"That was a warm-up!" she yelled.

"Strike one!" Dylan replied.

Aggie grumbled under her breath but put the bat back up and got ready to swing again. This time, she managed to hit the ball past Jac, who had to go running after it while Aggie booked it toward first base, jumping on top of the beanbag with a triumphant yell before heading toward second.

"Hey, watch the beanbag!" Taylor said. She didn't seem thrilled about Aggie getting a hit off of her pitch. "We don't want one of them exploding again!"

"Beans *everywhere*," Tink said. "It was a *disaster*."

But as Jac finally caught up to the ball and started to run back to the game, she could tell that something was wrong. Aggie's pace was slowing down until she was standing perfectly still between second and third base.

"Aggs?" Dylan called, pulling off her catcher's mask and looking toward her friend. "You all right?"

Jac felt a surge of protection when Dylan said that. She should be the one asking, not Dylan, but for some reason it was hard to talk, scary to see Aggie standing so still, even as all the other girls started to move toward her.

"I found one!" Josephine yelled, followed by "Oh, wait, no, I didn't."

But Jac wasn't paying attention to any of that. Instead, she was looking at Aggie, who was looking down at her shorts, and at the dark red stain that was starting to spread there.

"Oh my God," Aggie said, and when she looked up at Jac, her eyes were wide. "Oh my God."

"Is this . . . is this, like, the first time?" Jac said, jogging over to her. She had always been the mysterious twin, at least by her count, but what if Aggie was the one who had been keeping secrets from her?

And then Aggie's lip started to tremble.

"No, don't be embarrassed!" Jac said as Aggie's eyes grew bigger and bigger. "It's totally fine; it's normal." She tried to think of everything she could say so that Aggie didn't freak out. "It's awesome, in fact!"

"What's going . . . ? Oh. *Oh.*" Tink had arrived on the scene. "Aggie, is this your first time?"

Aggie nodded just as her eyes spilled over, and soon all the girls (minus Josephine, which was definitely for the best) were gathered around her, trying to comfort her.

"It's okay," Dylan said, patting Aggie's shoulder. "Trust me, it feels weird at first but you get used to it."

Jac nodded, avoiding looking at Aggie, suddenly at a loss that she couldn't help her sister. She couldn't remember a time when Aggie had done something first, had gone down a path that Jac had never traveled before. It was weird to feel that way about something she couldn't even control, and even weirder that she felt upset about it.

"It's really fine, Aggie," Jac said instead, trying to sound like she knew what she was talking about. "Seriously."

"I have a pad in my bag," Marnie said. "I mean, I haven't started yet or anything, but just in case."

"Aggie," Adriana said gently. "Um, you do know what's happening, right? Like, you don't think you're *dying* or something?"

"Of *course* I know what's happening," Aggie said, wiping at her eyes. "I got my stupid period." She burst into a fresh set of tears. "These are Jac's shorts, too! And why am I even crying?!"

"You know I don't care about that," Jac said quietly, and she really didn't.

"Dylan's right. The first time feels really strange," Adriana tried to reassure her. "But it's actually not that bad."

Aggie sniffled and wiped at her eyes on her shirtsleeve. Next to her, Taylor was quiet but sympathetic, patting her shoulder, while Adriana ran over to her bag and came back with a small pack of tissues, passing them to her friend.

"Are you worried about telling your dads?" Tink asked, biting her lower lip.

"No, no, they're cool. They practically have a period gift basket in every single bathroom in our house." Aggie sighed and wiped her eyes with Adri's tissues, which had tiny kittens printed all over them.

Jac nodded in agreement. Going through that conversation with their dads had been both boring and agonizing. "I don't think we're going to have to buy any supplies for at least the next fifteen years," Jac added. "I think our dads bought out Costco."

Aggie tried to smile, but it was wobbly. "They're probably going to want to celebrate, and they're going to say it's so amazing, and knowing them, they'll probably have a *cake* or something—"

"Cake?" piped up a hopeful little voice from left field.

"And they'll probably congratulate me on being a *woman*."

All the girls shuddered at that. "Parents are so awkward," Tink said. "Seriously. They have no idea what they're doing."

"They just act like all these normal things are so special," Jac said, trying to prop up Aggie on her other side. Was this what happened when you got your period, you started crying all over the place? Jac was suddenly a little less excited about getting hers.

"Well, maybe they think that *you're* special," Taylor said, and Aggie fell quiet at that.

"I guess," she said after a minute.

"What about cake?" a voice shouted from over by the clover patch.

"Like your dad told me," Dylan said, "you should talk to them. You're their kid and they love you, even if they do something totally boneheaded like get you a cake."

"Are we having cake now?!"

"And if you want to act like it's just another day, that's fine, too. But you should probably tell at least one of your dads."

"Are you embarrassed to tell them?" Jac asked. She could understand that. Feelings were so weird these days. There was nothing to have been embarrassed about, of course, but it was something new, and Aggie didn't do well with change.

"I'm not *embarrassed*," Aggie said. "It's just more like things are changing, you know? And they won't ever go back to how they were and it makes me feel sad and not like celebrating."

All the girls nodded at that.

"Well, let's move out of the sun at least," Adriana said, pulling her "Making Lemonade" T-shirt away from her. "It's boiling hot out here today. It's worse than summer, even."

The eight of them moved in a little pod toward the shade, Aggie at the center of their circle. "I guess I should change," she started to say, but before anyone else could offer up a fresh set of clothes, Josephine came over with a round mouth and huge eyes.

"Ohhh," she whispered. "You got your blood period."

It took a second, but Aggie was the first one to burst out laughing, quickly followed by the rest of the girls. "Josephine!" she cried, putting her arm around the youngest team member's shoulders. "You can just say 'period.' You don't have to elaborate. We understand."

"I have plenty of shorts upstairs," Tink said, heading toward their front porch. "C'mon."

"And you can have my emergency pad," Marnie added. "I'll help you figure it out. There are all these tabs and everything."

Josephine watched them wander off, then looked up at Jac. "But what kind of cake is it?" she asked.

"No cake," Jac said. "How about a granola bar instead?"

"Fine." Josephine pouted. "But when I get my blood period, I want *everybody* to bring me cake."

"You got it, kid," Jac said. "Cake for everyone."

After Aggie changed into a pair of Tink's pink capris, after Marnie had handed over her emergency pad and she and Dylan talked Aggie into using it through the bathroom door ("Wings are important, just trust me!" Dylan told her), and after Josephine had been consoled with one half of an oats-and-honey granola bar, Jac was sitting next to Aggie on Tink's patio, drinking a can of La Croix. "You know," Jac said, raising the can to her mouth, "for all the times that we meet up, we don't really practice all that much."

"Something's always happening," Aggie agreed, drinking from her own can and watching Josephine do cartwheels on the lawn under Adriana's watchful eye ("Point your toes! No, point them the *other* way!"). Aggie's eyes were still a little puffy but she wasn't crying anymore, so Jac took that as a win. "Good thing we have so much innate talent."

Jac snorted at that. "So."

"So." Aggie sighed. "I feel weird. I feel like I'm leaking."

"Well, I mean, you kind of are," Jac said, and when Aggie cracked a small smile, she grinned, too. "Does it hurt?"

"Not really. My stomach kind of hurts, but it's not bad." Aggie took another breath and watched as Josephine tumbled to the ground. "She really has zero athletic ability."

"Not a single shred," Jac agreed.

"Jac? Could you . . . ? I'll tell dads, I promise, but not yet. I want to just, I don't know, figure out how I feel about things first, okay?"

"Of course," Jac said, even though that didn't sit entirely right with her. They always told their dads everything, even that time when Jack the Rat once again escaped his cage and managed to eat his way through nearly a dozen of their dads' socks. Jack the Rat was lucky to be alive after that, for several reasons.

Jac was about to say something else when the screen door slammed open. She assumed it was Marnie or Tink or Dylan.

It was not.

It was Finn.

"Oh!" she said before she could stop herself.

He glanced down at her, and Jac felt her entire body flush. Why did she always say stupid stuff around him? Why did she never sound sophisticated and mature and grown up?

It got worse.

"Tink gave us these," she said, holding up her La Croix.

"Cool," Finn said. "I didn't think you stole them."

Jac laughed at that, too long and too loud, and ignored the strange look that Aggie was giving her. "Yeah, we're definitely not thieves," she said, smiling brightly.

"Are you okay?" Aggie whispered, and Jac gave her a hard elbow to the ribs.

"Hey, Joey!" Finn yelled across the yard to where Josephine was mid-cartwheel. "You have to come in—Grandma said so!"

"I do not answer to that name!" she yelled back,

her shirt over her head and then falling back down as she stood up. *"Phinneas."*

Finn groaned and said something that sounded like "Ugh, sisters" under his breath before sighing. "Josephine! Come inside."

"That's better," she said primly, running over and then skipping every other porch step before heading into the house. "Bye!" she called. "Don't forget my cake, okay?"

"Cake?" Finn asked.

"It's a long story," Jac said. She liked Finn, *really* liked him, but she was not about to explain the whole "my sister got her period and I think our dads might give her a cake" drama of the afternoon to a boy.

"OKAY?" Josephine yelled, and Jac gave her a thumbs-up before she disappeared inside.

"So you're from San Francisco," Finn said, and it took Jac a few beats before she realized that he was talking to her.

"Yes!" she said, with entirely too much enthusiasm. Next to her, Aggie took a very exaggerated and loud sip of her soda, her eyes wide over the rim of the can.

"I mean, yeah, we're from the Bay Area," she said, silently willing her heart to slow down and not race ahead of her. "We grew up there." She always thought "the Bay Area" sounded so sophisticated, and she hoped Finn felt the same way.

"Cool," Finn said. "I really want to work for a start-up one day."

"Cool," Jac replied.

"Cool," Finn said again.

Jac was about to say something else, *anything* else, but just then the carbonated fizz from the can went up her nose and she started to splutter and cough. Aggie gave her a few hard raps on the back, and by the time she was able to speak again, Finn had gone inside.

"Yikes," Aggie said. "You sounded like you were dying."

Jac wiped her watery eyes and threw her sister a dirty look. "Thanks," she said. "That's very helpful."

Her unsuccessful flirting attempts smoldered for the rest of the evening, as did all of her feelings about Aggie's big day, so she did what all siblings do when they're feeling cranky and out of sorts: she took it out on her sister. "Your elbow is too close to me," Jac grumbled at one point at dinner, and Aggie blinked at her in clear confusion.

"I can't exactly move my elbow to a different part of my body," she replied.

"Ugh, it's just annoying," Jac said, shifting on the bench so she could scoot away from her sister, and missing the hurt look on Aggie's face. "And why do we have to have spinach in *everything*?"

"Because we enjoy making our children feel

miserable," her dad said pleasantly, passing Aggie a plate of corn on the cob. "And we want to make sure that your bones don't disintegrate when you're fifty years old and you have to eat Jell-O for the rest of your lives."

Jac scowled at her plate, knowing the tone in her dad's voice. It was the "I'm being pleasant now but I'm going to be a lot less pleasant if you keep being a grump" voice. She took the corn from Aggie and helped herself to an ear. Then she poked at her spinach-filled salad and pointedly ate around all the greens, leaving them in a sad, shriveled pile at the bottom of her bowl.

"Can I be excused?" she asked.

"No," her papa said, sounding equally pleasant and irritated. "You're going to help me in the garden after dinner."

"But it's too hot," she whined. Jac could feel herself getting irritated in her own skin, her attitude starting to annoy even herself, but she could never quite figure out how to rein it in, how to calm down and not feel so frustrated.

Next to her, Aggie was eating all of her salad without complaint. Jac felt like giving her a pinch, but she wisely decided against that.

"It's too hot," she said again. "I feel like my skin is going to melt right off my body."

"Like in Indiana Jones?" her papa said, and his

joking comment made her even more irritable.

"And it's, like, eighty degrees out," her dad added, gesturing with his fork.

"And this is one of the last few weeks of sun after dinner," her papa said. "So we have to plant the fall bulbs now."

"They're just going to die anyway," Jac said, crossing her arms over her chest.

"Maybe so," her papa said. "But the fun is in the work, not the success!"

Jac had her doubts.

After dinner, while their dad and Aggie cleaned up the kitchen while listening to BTS on the Bluetooth speaker, Jac trudged outside and took her place next to her papa, who handed her a small trowel and a pair of gardening gloves. "Okay, Miss Mopey," he said. "What's up?"

"If you want me to talk to you, calling me 'Miss Mopey' is probably not the best way to do that," Jac said, taking the trowel from him and shoving it into the dirt.

"Okay, that's fair, I apologize," he said, and Jac immediately felt 90 percent of her crankiness leave her body. Her dads were always good about apologizing when they said or did something wrong. It was one of Jac's favorite things about them. "So why the grumps?"

Jac used her trowel to fling some dirt around. When you're cranky, making a mess is always very satisfying. "Nothing," she said.

"I may not be an expert," he said, "but I've found that when you or Aggie say that it's nothing, it's definitely *something*."

Jac scowled at the hole she was digging. "Can't it just be something without having to always talk about it?" she said. "When you're cranky after work, I don't follow you around and ask you a bunch of questions about it."

Her papa didn't respond. Instead, he sat on his heels and pushed his sunglasses back up on his head, looking at her. "Jac," he said. "What's going on with you?"

"It's stupid Finn!" she burst out. "I was talking to him and he was like, 'Cool,' and then I was like, 'Cool,' and then I choked on my soda and couldn't talk and Aggie was just sitting there and being *annoying* like she always is."

"Finn?" her papa asked.

"Tink's older brother," Jac admitted. Now that she had confessed, she felt small, like a scolded little kid.

"Ohhhh," her papa said, then sat down next to her in the dirt. "It's a boy."

"Why do you have to say it like that?" Jac said. "It's a *boy*, like I met a wizard or something! And how do you know it's even a boy? I could like a *girl* named Finn, too, you know."

"Very true," her papa said, wrapping his arms around his knees. "But this particular Finn is a boy, yes?"

Jac nodded begrudgingly. "Finn does identify as male, yes."

"Got it. And you like him?"

Jac nodded again, feeling the wave of embarrassment wash over her once more. "It's like whenever he's around, I get stupid."

"Yep," he said. "Sounds like a crush."

"Even the word 'crush' is bad," Jac said. "Nothing survives being crushed."

"I think you have a future as a songwriter," her papa said. "But in the meantime, this Finn—"

"His name is just Finn, Dad."

"Does he like you?"

"Of course not!" Jac said. "Because I always act like a total doofus around him! And even if I'm being normal, everyone around me is acting like a doofus. There's always drama happening and Josephine's doing a million cartwheels and talking about penguins or whatever."

"Jac," her papa said, sounding fond. "I've literally known you every single minute that you've been on the planet, and I don't think you've ever been capable of acting like a doofus."

It was a strange compliment, but Jac would take it.

"Even at your preschool recital," he continued. "You would sing all the songs, but you refused to do the little dances they taught you because you said they were, and this is a direct quote, 'immature.' You were barely five years old. Trust me, you are not a doofus."

Jac tried not to smile at that. She failed. "Mrs. Maynard was so annoyed."

"She was not a fan," her papa agreed. "Good thing it was your last day."

Jac let out a long, low breath and shoved her hair out of her eyes. It was getting longer. She needed a trim. "I just don't know what to do when I see him," she said. "But whatever I do, it feels wrong."

Her papa nodded at that. "You know," he said, "when I first met your dad, on our first date, I spilled a glass of wine all over myself. Red wine."

Jac winced. "Yikes."

"Yep. I wanted the ground to open up and swallow me whole, I was so embarrassed."

"Was this the date where he was thirty minutes late?"

"Indeed it was. Thank you for remembering that very important detail. But my point is, we're married now, and we have two pretty cool kids, so maybe it wasn't the worst thing that happened. You know?"

"I snorted La Croix up my nose right in front of Finn," Jac admitted.

"Ow," her papa said.

"Exactly." She sighed. "And I don't know what to say or what to ask him. I feel like I can't be myself, but I don't know who else to be."

Her papa smiled a little. "Oh, kiddo, you've got it bad."

"I do." She said it sadly. "I think I need ice cream to feel better."

He barked out a laugh at that and gestured to the flower bed. "Dig first," he said. "And tell me more about this Finn."

"*Finn*, Papa. Just Finn."

"Just Finn. Got it."

It didn't take long for Jac to fill him in on every single detail about Finn, mostly because she didn't know that much. He wore checkered Vans and was pretty nice to his sisters, he had hair that fell across his forehead like an ocean wave, he was pretty tan and had one crooked front tooth that Jac hoped he would never get braces to fix. Her papa listened as he planted fall bulbs and as Jac scooped dirt gently over them, patting them into their new homes. It was nice being outside at sunset, she had to admit, and as she worked and dug and talked, she felt all of that tightness leaving her body, making her feel like her normal Jac self again.

"And what does Aggie think about all this?" her

papa said, passing her a bulb with exceptionally long roots.

Jac was quiet as she pushed it down into the earth. "I don't talk to Aggie about it," she said quietly. "She doesn't understand. She *wouldn't* understand."

"Have you at least tried?" he asked. His voice was as quiet as hers.

Jac shook her head. "I just know," she said. "We're . . . Sometimes Aggie and I, we look a lot alike but we think a lot different. We *are* a lot different." *Especially now*, she thought to herself.

"You always have been," her papa said. "And that's okay. You're a good team together, but it's okay to do different things. All sisters do."

Jac shrugged. "I just always feel like . . . I don't know, like I'm betraying her if I'm not exactly like her."

He smiled ruefully. "The pressure of being a twin."

"Seriously."

"Well, for what it's worth, I like that you two are so different," her papa said. "Makes things exciting around here. Imagine if we had two of the exact same kids." He shuddered. "It'd be like a horror movie. Like those twins in *The Shining*."

"You won't let Aggie and I watch that movie," Jac pointed out.

"And rightly so," he said. "I didn't sleep for a

month after I saw it." He shuddered again, which only made Jac want to watch that movie even more. "But my point is that you and Aggie are different and you don't have to feel bad about that. And this Finn—"

"Papa."

"Okay, that one was intentional, sorry. But *Finn* sounds like a cool kid. Anybody who wears checkered Vans is a friend of mine."

Jac rolled her eyes but felt secretly pleased on the inside. Her papa had been a skater kid growing up in San Francisco and still had a *Thrasher* hoodie that he liked to wear around on Sunday mornings. Jac and Aggie wouldn't allow him to wear it outside of the house, though.

"What do you think?" he said. "Should we go inside? It's blazing hot out here." He swore under his breath, and Jac politely pretended not to hear him. "All it would take is one spark . . ." he said before trailing off, and Jac pretended not to hear that part, too.

"Sure," she said. "Can we have ice cream?"

"Mayhaps," he said. "Did you do your homework?"

"It's not due until Friday, and it's only Tuesday."

He started to say something, then stopped. "Well, from one procrastinator to another, okay. But start it by tomorrow, all right? Don't be like your papa who's always stressing out at the last minute."

"Kay," Jac said, then stood up and started brushing dirt off her gloved hands. "Do you think these are going to grow?" she asked, gesturing toward their garden bed.

"Only one way to find out," he said, and Jac didn't shrug him off when he put his hand on her shoulder as they walked back to the house.

It felt nice.

CHAPTER 13

AGGIE

Aggie lay in bed for a long time that night, feeling numb, her sister's words reverberating around in her brain.

"She doesn't understand."

"She *wouldn't* understand."

"We look a lot alike, but we think a lot different."

It wasn't like any of this was news to Aggie, but still, it burned something deep inside her to hear her twin sister say those words out loud. One minute she had been dancing to BTS in the kitchen with her dad (whose dancing moves were why he was never allowed to dance outside of their house), and she had been putting one of their big mixing bowls over by the back screen door, and she hadn't meant to eavesdrop, but as she heard Jac's voice, she could feel the bowl getting lighter and lighter in her hands, until it was like she wasn't even holding it at all.

What wouldn't Aggie understand?

Aggie had a sneaking suspicion that it had to do with Tink's brother, Finn, and the way Jac's face flushed and turned pink whenever he suddenly appeared. Aggie had never seen her sister get so flustered before, and the way Jac smiled at Finn made Aggie realize that Jac never smiled like that at anyone else, not even Jack the Rat. And if that was the case, then Jac was right.

Aggie didn't understand.

Finn was just some boy, and sure, he had nice hair or whatever, but he was Tink and Josephine's *brother*. She didn't understand why Jac always looked like she was about to swallow her tongue whenever he was around, and not understanding made Aggie secretly feel like Jac was moving further and further away from her, traveling in one direction while Aggie was suddenly being jerked onto a different road entirely, having her own separate journey.

It made her feel awful inside, small and alone and confused.

And when Aggie felt awful, she got mean.

When she woke up on Saturday morning, it felt like she had a brick on her chest, a hot brick filled with bitterness and anger. "Hey," Jac said, knocking on her bedroom door and coming in without even asking. "C'mon, we're going to be late for practice."

"Why do we even call it practice?" Aggie grumbled, rolling over to bury her face in the cool spot of the pillow. "We hit two balls, and then someone's personal drama interrupts everything."

"Wow, okay, Miss Cheerful," Jac said, using a voice that made Aggie want to give her a pinch. "Well, I'll be at practice, and you're welcome to join me. Dads!" she yelled down the hall. "Be careful this morning. Aggie's cranky!"

Nothing made Aggie crankier than someone telling her that she was cranky. "Get out," she said, throwing the no-longer-cool pillow in her sister's direction. "I didn't even give you permission to come in."

Jac dodged the pillow in a way that Aggie found supremely irritating, then waltzed out of the room.

Jac was right: they did have practice, and despite the fact that Aggie was not wrong and the word "practice" barely applied to their latest meetups, she still dragged herself out of bed, washed her face and brushed her teeth, wrangled her hair into a semblance of a ponytail, and pulled on shorts and a T-shirt. When she caught her reflection in the mirror, she tried to smile, but then got frustrated and instead stuck her tongue out at her own image, not even willing to be nice to herself.

It's going to be a long day, she thought.

Aggie had no idea how right she was.

"Okay!" Tink said, clapping her hands. "Before we start practice, I have an announcement!"

Aggie caught Jac's eye and gave her an "I told you so" look, which Jac promptly ignored.

"I've decided on our group costumes for Halloween this year!"

"Why do you always get to decide?" Adriana grumbled. It was barely eleven in the morning, but the sun was already blazing down and there wasn't even a hint of a breeze. Aggie wasn't the only one who was cranky that morning. All the girls were hot and sweaty, and they hadn't even started playing yet. "Like I was saying!" Tink cried, giving Adriana a dirty look. "I've come up with the perfect group costume." Her cheeks were flushed pink, and Aggie wasn't sure if it was because of the heat or her excitement.

"I'm a Peeeeeeeaaaaaaach!" Josephine screeched.

"Josephine!" Tink said. "C'mon, you're ruining the surprise."

"Sorry," she said, not sounding sorry at all.

"Anyway," Tink said, and blew her bangs off her forehead. "I think we should all be Rockford Peaches. You know, like in the movie *A League of Their Own*!"

There was a brief pause.

"It's all about a girls' softball team!" Tink cried. "It's perfect!"

"I don't even know what a Rockford Peach is," Dylan added. "I never saw that movie. And besides, I was going to be the Little Mermaid."

"Again?" Marnie said.

"The costume still fits." Dylan shrugged. "And I like the wig. It's very dramatic."

"Like mother, like daughter," Marnie teased, and Aggie waited for Dylan to get upset, but all she did was playfully swat at Marnie and then chase her around until they both collapsed on Tink's front lawn, giggling.

"I think it's a perfect costume!" Aggie said just as Jac added, "Do we *have* to do a group costume?"

"Yeah," Dylan said. "Seriously, this is probably the last year I can be Ariel. My mom says I'm going through a growth spurt."

"Dylan, every year you hop all over the neighborhood in your mermaid tail, and every year you complain how uncomfortable and hot it is," Tink said. "And it's supposed to be one hundred degrees on Halloween this year."

"Global warming is real," Adriana said, shaking her head.

"Why is it so hot?" Marnie moaned. "We should all go as Olympic swimmers and just wear bathing suits."

Tink frowned again, and Aggie could tell she was

annoyed by all the distractions. "My mom can order the costumes for us," she said. "She found them online for super cheap, and they come in a bunch of sizes."

Jac raised her hand like she was asking her teacher a question. "But I think I want to be something else."

"Same," Adriana said.

"I'll go as whatever," Taylor said. "I just want to make sure that we hit up Warbler Way because they have the full-size candy bars."

"We'll probably get more candy if we go as a group," Tink pointed out. "Parents and adults love the group thing."

"There's no crying in baseball!" Josephine said.

"Exactly," Tink said. "Plus we can promote our team and practices."

"What team?" Aggie said, and everyone turned to look at her. "We don't even play actual games. We just hang out in the street and run around and tag the neighbor's mailbox."

She regretted her words immediately once she saw Tink's face fall. She was definitely annoyed with Jac, but hurting Tink felt like kicking a puppy. "I mean," she said quickly, "I love it and I always have fun. But we're not really a *real* team."

Josephine frowned and put her arm around her sister's waist. "You're being mean," she said. "That's not allowed in baseball, either."

"Actually," Marnie started to say, but quickly shut up once Jac shook her head at her.

"What does 'real' even mean?" Taylor said. "So we aren't part of a league or play in actual games. We're still a team. That's what matters."

That seemed to comfort Tink somewhat, and Aggie slunk toward the back of the group. She hated when she got like this, nitpicky and frustrated and like the world was both too big and too small. "Well, I'm fine with a group costume," she said. "Whatever. Our dads can Venmo your mom."

"I . . ." Adriana shifted her gaze from left to right. "I might want to go as something else, like Jac said."

"What?" Tink cried. "Since when?"

"I don't know. I was just thinking about it!" Adriana said. "My older sister has this really cool costume and she can't wear it anymore and it fits me perfectly and . . ." She trailed off.

"The Rockford Peaches are really cool, too," Tink said, and Aggie could tell that she was still hurt.

"I haven't even seen the movie, but I'll wear it," Dylan said. "But I'm also going to wear my Ariel wig, too."

"Fine, whatever," Tink said.

"Trixiebelle!"

All the girls' heads turned as they heard someone shuffle out onto the front porch, and Aggie saw an older woman with a walker come out into the sun. "Did you put on sunscreen?" the woman cried. "It's so hot out today!"

Trixiebelle?!

"Grandma!" Tink yelled. "Yes! I'm fine!"

Josephine was giggling behind her hands. "Trixiebelle," she murmured, her voice muffled by her fingers.

Aggie and Jac exchanged a loaded glance. *Trixiebelle?!* Was it possible that someone could have a worse name than either one of them? Aggie already liked Tink just fine before, but now she felt a special bond with her. Sometimes having creative parents was really a curse.

"Make sure you hydrate, Trixiebelle!" Tink's grandma continued, and Tink looked like she wished the earth would open up and swallow her whole. "You too, Josephine! Your mother will have my head if you two end up dehydrated."

"Grandma, you're so dramatic!" Tink said even as Josephine collapsed on the ground pretended to writhe like a fish out of water. "Josephine, get up, seriously."

"Hi, Mrs. Alvarez!" Taylor called, waving at her, and Tink's grandma grinned and waved back.

"Hey there, Taylor!" she yelled. "Tell your mom and dad to come over for dinner soon, okay?"

"Got it," Taylor said.

By the time her grandma went back inside, Tink was staring at the ground, her cheeks blazing. This time, Aggie knew it wasn't because of the heat. "*Trixie*-belle," Aggie said. "That's rough."

"My mom and dad got really creative with all three of our names," Tink said defensively.

Aggie and Jac exchanged another loaded glance. "Same with us," Aggie said. "I think our dads had a collective stroke right before they named both of us. That's the only explanation."

"What, you're not Aggie and Jac?"

"I thought you were named after a rat," Josephine added, and Tink wisely gave her sister a "please stop talking" nudge.

Aggie sighed and waited for Jac to nod at her before continuing. "We're actually named after plants," she said. "Our dad's a florist and landscape architect whatever, and apparently, the hospital where we were born had all these trees and flowers outside, and right after we were born he looked out the hospital window and . . ."

Aggie sighed and Jac took over.

"He saw a bunch of jacaranda trees," she said. "And . . . some agapanthus."

It took a few seconds before the realization hit the other girls, but when it did, fully half of them gasped and covered their mouths with their hands.

"No!" Adriana said.

"I think they're pretty!" Taylor said. "They're both so nice and purple."

"I'm named after my grandma's sister who died!" Josephine beamed.

"At least you don't sound like a Disney character!" Tink said.

"Nobody wins this game!" Aggie protested. "Do you know what it's like being named Aga*panthus*?"

"At least no one else has your name?" Taylor said helpfully. "You're never going to be Agapanthus P. in class, right? There were five Taylors in my fourth-grade class."

"I wish I was!" Aggie said. "At least Jacaranda sounds glamorous."

"'Jacaranda' sounds like someone who could be on my mom's show," Dylan said, and Jac visibly brightened at that.

"I think we should be allowed to name our parents," Tink said. "If they can name us, it's only fair."

"I'm going to name Mommy 'Sparkly Unicorn' because she's beautiful," Josephine said dreamily, then saw a monarch butterfly and wandered off.

"Okay, so anyway," Marnie said, putting her oven-gloved hands on her hips, "interesting names and delusional parents aside, we're doing Rockford Peaches, right?" She looked expectantly at each of the girls, as if daring them to say otherwise.

"Yes," Tink said. "All for one and one for all."

"I literally still have no idea what you're talking about," Dylan said.

But Aggie couldn't help but notice that Jac and Adriana were very, very quiet.

Two weeks later, Halloween rolled around, and it was boiling hot outside.

"Ugh, I feel like this costume is strangling me," Aggie said, tugging at her pink skirted jumpsuit. "Is this seriously what they had to wear back in the olden days?"

"The *olden* days," her dad scoffed.

"Well, polyester isn't exactly a breathable fabric," her other dad said. He was carrying a huge plastic jack-o'-lantern full of fun-size M&M's over to the front door, warned by their neighbors that trick-or-treaters tended to come out in droves. "We're not running out of candy on our first Halloween in the neighborhood!" he said in Target last weekend, hoisting bag after bag of chocolate into their cart while Aggie and Jac pretended that they belonged to some other family. "Not on my watch!"

Aggie frowned again, adjusting her ponytail out of her baseball cap. "Where's Jac?" she said. "We have to go over to Tink's now or we're going to be late."

The sky outside was pink and shimmering from heat, and it reminded Aggie of some of those '80s sci-fi movies her dads had let her and Jac watch last year. It seemed more like a film set than an actual neighborhood, and Aggie felt a tiny poke of something settle in her stomach. It wasn't fear, it wasn't anxiety, it was just . . . *something.*

Something not good.

So she obviously ignored it.

"Jac!" she yelled up the stairs.

"Can you please not yell?" her dad said, and if he thought Aggie didn't see him swipe a few M&M's packs from the jack-o'-lantern, he was sorely mistaken. "Just go up and get your sister."

Instead, Aggie reached for her phone and texted Jac: "COME ONNNNNNNNN."

"No, I meant—" her dad said, then rubbed his forehead. "Like, go upstairs and actually tell your sister to come downstairs. Don't just text her. I swear, I'm going to take you both to Amish country and raise you without electricity."

"That would be more of a punishment for *you,*" Aggie said, glancing in the front hallway mirror and adjusting her hat again.

Her papa snickered. "Well, she's not wrong," he said when her dad gave him a dirty look. "Here, toss me some M&M's."

There were footsteps upstairs, and then Aggie saw a black patent-leather Mary Jane set foot on the top step. That was definitely not appropriate footwear for a Rockford Peach, and Aggie felt her heart sink as she watched Jac descend the stairs dressed in dark knee-high stockings, a black lace dress, and a black wig on her head that had been parted into two braids and thick bangs.

She was a perfect Wednesday Addams.

"How do I look?" she said.

"Amazing!" Aggie's dad said, clearly unaware that he was being a total backstabber right then. "That costume looks great on you!"

"I thought you were going to be a Peach," Aggie said darkly. Next to Jac, her own costume felt dumb and babyish, and she had the urge to run upstairs and rip it off and never go trick-or-treating again.

But candy.

"I told Tink back when she first said that that I wanted to be something else," Jac said, sounding both proud and defensive. "I don't have to go along with what everyone else does. Right, Dads?"

"Hear, hear," their dad said, and Aggie had to resist the urge to roll her eyes. Her dads were total suckers for the whole "I'm an independent person" thing, and Jac clearly knew that, too.

"Yeah, it's just that, you know, we're a team?"

Aggie said. "Both on Halloween and otherwise?"

"Just because I'm wearing a different costume doesn't mean I'm not part of the team," Jac shot back, and now she sounded purely defensive. "And it's one dumb holiday, Aggie. You can wear whatever costume you want to, too, you know. It's a free country."

"I *am* wearing the costume I want to wear," Aggie said, then adjusted her hat again. She could already feel sweat breaking out along her hairline under the brim, and she hoped she wouldn't feel too gross by the end of the night. "C'mon, we're going to be late."

After promising their parents they would keep their phones on the entire time, and after swearing up and down that they would text every thirty minutes after the sun set, and after letting them take at least a dozen photos on their phones, Aggie and Jac set out for the two-block walk to Tink's house. The silence between them was heavy and thick, both of them irritated with the other one. It wasn't how Aggie wanted to spend her Halloween, and she thought glumly of all the Halloweens where she and Jac had gone out in matching outfits: ballerinas, princesses, puppy dogs. It had always been fun to look back at the photos and point out how cute they had looked together, but Aggie suspected that she wasn't going to want to remember this particular Halloween, not at all.

By the time they got to Tink's house, the sun was

starting to set and Aggie was sweating. "Hi!" Tink said, running out of the house in her matching costume. "Hi! Hi! Hi! Oh."

Jac shuffled nervously. "I wanted to do something else," she said before Tink could even say a word about her costume.

"Oh," Tink said again, and Aggie had that awful feeling that she had gotten back in fifth grade when the cool girls had sat together at lunch and she and her friends had sat at a different table. It wasn't that Aggie wanted to do anything different, or switch out her friends, or be an entirely different person, but it was the feeling that just by being herself, she was doing something wrong.

"You look nice," Jac said, clearly extending an olive branch, and Tink opened her mouth to say something, when Josephine came racing out of the house in her own Rockford Peach uniform.

"There's no crying in baseball!" she cried as she ran across the yard and flung her arms around Jac's waist, tilting her head back to look up at her. "Why are you dressed like my other grandma who died?"

"Oh geez," Tink sighed, then pulled her sister away from Jac before she could smear her candy-covered mouth all over her costume. "Sorry, our other grandma died before we were born and Josephine's kind of obsessed."

"I like it," Josephine added before she went to give Aggie a hug, a gesture that Aggie wasn't entirely upset about. "And *you* look like me!"

"I do!" Aggie agreed, hugging her back. At times like this, Aggie thought that it wouldn't have been the worst thing to have a little sister, someone to look up to her and admire her, rather than constantly *stabbing her in the back and being a traitor.*

Yep, Aggie was bitter.

"I'm a Peeeeaaaaaaach!" Josephine yelled, letting go of Aggie and racing toward Taylor and Marnie, both of whom were walking up in their own team costumes.

"Sorry, she snuck a few Pixy Stix when no one was looking, and well . . ." Tink gestured toward her sister, who was now doing cartwheels in a manic circle. "That's what happened."

Aggie was about to say something about how nice it was to have a sister *who looked up to you*, when an SUV pulled up to the curb and Adriana hopped out in her own unique costume.

"Oh, thank goodness," Jac muttered under her breath.

Adriana was wearing a black robe, a lace collar, a string of pearls, with fake lens-free glasses and her hair pulled back into a tight, slick bun. "Tink, don't even start with me!" she said before she was even out of the car. "I'm honoring Ruth Bader Ginsburg tonight, and nobody can make me do anything else."

"Can definitely confirm that last part!" her mom yelled cheerily from the driver's seat as Adriana scrambled out to the curb, and Aggie suspected that trying to parent a preteen entrepreneur was probably exhausting.

"Hey, Wednesday!" Adriana said, fist-bumping Jac and completely unaware of the drama she was creating. "You look great! Everyone looks so good!"

"I thought you were going to be a Peach," Tink said darkly from beneath the brim of her ball cap.

"I was, but things change," Adriana said. "RBG was a pioneer." She tucked a stray lock of hair back into her bun, then smiled. "It's just a costume, Tink. Don't overthink it."

Aggie was pretty sure that there was nothing worse than someone telling you not to be angry when you felt like your head was going to explode. And judging from the look on Tink's face, she felt the same way.

"Everyone looks great!" Marnie said, exchanging a quick glance with Jac.

"Yeah, for sure," Jac added. "What I like about our friendship is that we're all individuals, right?"

"Jac," Marnie sighed under her breath. "Rack it back a bit."

Jac just smiled, showing all of her teeth, which did nothing to make Aggie feel better.

Once Taylor and Dylan (who was absolutely wearing her Ariel wig) showed up in their own Peach costumes, the eight of them headed out for the full-size-candy-bar neighborhood a few blocks away. It was clear they weren't the only ones with that plan. As they got closer to the coveted houses, cars started to pull up, emptying out dozens of tiny Avengers and unicorns and cheerleaders and even a kid in an inflatable dinosaur costume.

"Wow, that's commitment," Jac said as they all watched the dinosaur try to exit the car without falling on their Jurassic face.

"People will do anything for free stuff." Adriana sighed. "Trust me."

Even with all the kids and with Tink's and Adriana's moms following along at an appropriate distance behind them and with full-size candy bar after full-size candy bar being deposited into Aggie's pillowcase, she still felt sad. Every time she looked at Jac with her dark dress and long braids, she felt as if, for the first time, she wasn't looking into a mirror, and it had nothing to do with their costumes. What if Jac wanted to always be different from her? What if Aggie was the different one? What if Jac decided that being like Aggie was the worst thing in the world?

What if Jac didn't want to be her sister anymore?

Aggie's heart became as heavy as her candy loot (full-size candy bars were amazing, but wow, were they heavy) as they walked around the large cul-de-sac. Some of the residents had put their cars at the base of the street so the kids could wander from house to house without worrying about traffic, and Aggie followed her friends as they zigzagged around the neighborhood, laughing and calling to each other.

At one point, Adriana lost a pearl earring and half the neighborhood stopped to find it, and at another point, Josephine tripped over a loose shoelace and was only consoled after someone pressed a tiny cardboard box of Nerds into her hand. "I'm sort of convinced she did that on purpose," Dylan muttered to Aggie, but Aggie was too focused on her own sister, who was talking to several boys with Adriana, who was re-inserting her earring.

As the sun set, they could hear sirens in the neighborhood, and Aggie saw both moms checking their phones, scrolling through notifications, their faces illuminated by the light from the screens. "Did you hear . . . ?" Tink's mom started to say, but then she turned her back to the girls and Aggie couldn't hear any more. At one point, a fire engine went up the street, its red lights flashing throughout the neighborhood, and Aggie felt that same shiver of something go up her spine.

She didn't know what exactly was wrong, but she knew that something was.

And as if that wasn't already stressful enough, Aggie kept watching Tink's face get gloomier and gloomier as they trudged around the block, her frown disappearing beneath the brim of her ball cap as she tugged it farther down over her eyes. At one point, she nearly fell over the curb and finally had to adjust the hat a bit, but she still looked upset. Aggie could understand it, of course. She herself was still cranky with Jac, the traitor. At least Josephine idolized Tink, thought the world revolved around her big sister, looked up to her and followed her everywhere.

Aggie tugged her own hat down and frowned as someone put raisins into her pillowcase.

When they were finally done, Tink slunk to the back of the group, uncharacteristically quiet as Josephine, on a sugar high from the last thirty minutes spent sneaking candy out of her bag, orbited around her while crowing happily. "What's with her?" Aggie heard Jac ask Adriana as they walked home. Aggie's feet hurt, the cleats were starting to rub a blister on her back heel, and there were still sirens going off in the neighborhood every few minutes.

"Which one?" Adriana responded.

"Tink," Jac whispered back. "Why is she being

so . . . not Tink-like? Is she really that mad about our costumes?"

Adriana sighed. "It would seem so."

"But why?" Jac scoffed a little, which made Aggie even angrier. "Who cares if we don't all dress alike? What's the big deal?"

Adriana glanced over her shoulder to make sure Tink couldn't hear before she continued. "She just likes to know what's going to happen," she said. "When she's not in charge of what's going on, it makes her anxious. Ever since their dad died right after Josephine was born, Tink likes to know what to expect. Which sucks, because that's impossible."

Aggie, who knew eavesdropping was bad but oh well, desperate times, et cetera, stayed quiet. She couldn't imagine not having one of her dads in her life. The thought was both impossible and terrifying, and she suddenly wished that she was back home listening to her dads putter around the house, working on their laptops and running the dishwasher and laughing at the TV.

"How did he die?" Jac asked.

"Car accident," Adriana replied. "I don't know a lot or even remember much. Tink and I and all of us were still in preschool, but I just remember all the adults crying and not being allowed to go to the memorial. That's when they moved into our neighborhood and into their grandma's house. And they just stayed." Adriana shrugged. "I heard my parents talking once, and they said that they didn't have much money, that her mom had to work two jobs at one point. I think things were really hard for them.

"That's why Tink started our little team," she added. "Because they couldn't afford all the uniforms and sign-up fees and everything for a Little League team, and if she signed up, then you know Josephine would be right behind her, and that's even more money. . . ." She trailed off.

Aggie had the sudden urge to rush over to Tink and give her a hug, but judging from the sulky look on Tink's face, that gesture would probably not be received well. Instead, she just hung back so she could walk next to her friend, tactfully avoiding Josephine's gyrating arms.

And besides, if there was one person who understood not liking being surprised by life, it was Aggie.

When they got back to Tink's house, some of their parents were already waiting for them, and Aggie saw her dad standing next to Taylor's dad, chatting and looking serious. Why did friendship always seem so easy for adults, Aggie thought in disgust. They talked about boring stuff like housing prices and taxes and gluten and boom! Best friends instantly! They never had to deal with Halloween drama.

"Hey!" their dad said. "I hope you got Twix for me!" He smiled, and despite her irritation, Aggie was glad to see him, healthy and in the flesh and very much not dead.

"We're an Almond Joy household," Taylor's dad said, and Taylor responded by making gagging noises.

"Coconut is disgusting," she said.

"Definitely your mother's child," her dad replied, but he was smiling.

Aggie was about to say something about how she was definitely on Taylor's side, but then Tink walked past all of them and stalked into the house, letting the screen door slam shut behind her. "I guess she doesn't like coconut, either?" Taylor's dad said.

"Please ignore my rudest child," Tink's mom said. "I don't know what's up with her tonight. But this one, I absolutely know what's up with her."

At that point, Josephine was just running in circles, making noises that sounded like a combination between a cat's purr and a dog's bark.

"Well, have fun with that," Aggie's dad said. He went to put his hand on top of Jac's head, but she ducked away. "Dad, respect the wig," she said.

"Oops, sorry, forgot," he said. He said his goodbyes to the other parents as he started to guide Jac and Aggie back home. At first Aggie had been annoyed that they couldn't have just walked home by themselves—they were almost thirteen after all—but now that it was dark out and the sirens seemed to be getting louder and louder, Aggie was glad to have him there.

"Sorry about your friend," her dad said. "Was she upset the whole night?"

"She just wanted everyone to wear the same costume," Jac said. "It's okay. She'll get over it."

Aggie shot her sister a dirty look. "You don't know that," she said. "Maybe she's really angry. Maybe she wants to dissolve the team."

"Maybe she does," Jac said, sounding equally irritated in the dark. "I guess we're all allowed to make our own choices."

"Hey, hey, c'mon," their dad said, now walking in between them. He didn't have his glasses on, so Aggie wasn't sure if it was to separate her or Jac or because he couldn't see well at night without them. "There's no crying in baseball, am I right?"

"Ugh, *Dad*," Aggie said. "Read the room."

"Wow, tough crowd," her dad replied.

When they got back to their house, Aggie could tell that something was off. Their neighbors' car was in the driveway, the garage open, and the neighbors were loading some suitcases and boxes into the trunk. "What are they doing?" Aggie asked. "Are they going on vacation?"

Their dad cleared his throat before responding.

"Um, so we all got a warning from the local fire department while you two were out with your friends, saying that we should get ready to go in case of an evacuation order."

"Evacuation?" Jac repeated. "Like, we have to leave our house?"

"Is it because of the fires?" Aggie asked, and just as she said that, an exceptionally warm breeze blew across her face. Despite its heat, it still made her shiver.

"Yes," her dad said. "Papa and I packed up a few things, and you two should probably put together a bag, too. But don't worry, we're just being extra cautious. Better to be safe than sorry, right?"

Aggie could hear the tightness in his voice, though, and all three of them watched as the neighbors slammed their trunk shut, hopped into the car and started the engine. "Where would we go, though?" Aggie said, not liking how small her voice sounded.

"A hotel," her dad replied. "But again, don't worry. Papa and I are in charge, and we have it under control, okay?" He squeezed Aggie's shoulder. He probably heard how small her voice sounded, too.

"Okay," Aggie said, but she didn't feel entirely certain about it. And judging by the uncertain look on Jac's face, she was feeling unsure as well.

When they got to the front door, both girls tried to walk through it at the same time, their shoulders bumping together. "Ow!" Aggie cried.

"I barely touched you!" Jac said.

"You literally shoved me into the doorjamb!"

Their papa came around the corner, holding a small bag of Whoppers. "Whoa!" he said. "What's going on? Why is everyone yelling?"

"Because she's rude!" Aggie said, glowering at Jac.

"Well, she's being a baby!" Jac said. "She's mad I wore a different costume than her!"

"I am not!" Aggie said, and hated how much she sounded like a whiny baby just then. Everything about the night suddenly felt too tight, too hot, too much.

"Jac's being bullied at school!" she said.

"What?!" their dads cried at the same time, both of them whipping around to look at Jac.

"Jacaranda, is that true?" her dad demanded.

"Why didn't you tell us?"

Jac looked like a tiny volcano about to erupt. "Well, why don't you ask Aggie why she didn't tell you that she got her period!"

"Jac!" Aggie screamed.

"WHAT?!" their dads said again, this time whirling to look at Aggie.

"Is *that* true?" their papa asked.

"Yes!" Aggie admitted. "I just didn't want to tell

you because I knew you'd make a big huge deal out of it and probably get a whole cake or something, so I told Jac not to tell you—"

"You started it!" Jac cried.

"A cake?" their dad said, then looked at their papa. "Were we supposed to get a cake now for this?"

Their papa held up his hands in defeat. "I have no idea. The rules keep changing on these things."

"Well, if Aggie had kept her mouth shut—" Jac yelled, but just then, their papa stepped in between them, hands up.

"This stops," he said in a voice that he rarely used, "right now."

Both girls immediately quieted down. It took a lot to make their dads angry, and at this moment, neither one of them looked thrilled.

"Go upstairs and get ready for bed," their papa said. "We'll discuss this in the morning, both of you."

The girls got ready for bed in silence, taking turns in the bathroom even though there were two sinks in there. Aggie pulled off her now-sweaty costume and tossed it into the laundry, preferring to never see it again, and pulled on her most comfortable pajamas. It felt weird to have the air-conditioning running on Halloween night but she was grateful for it, and then she glanced around her bedroom, trying to figure out what to pack just in case. Her stuffed animals? Her clothes? Would she need to pack more pads? What about all of her Magic Tree House books? She hadn't even read them in years, but she still felt attached to them. Suddenly, it felt like every single thing was important, that there wasn't a bag or suitcase big enough to hold everything that Aggie loved and needed.

She finally put some clothes and stuffed animals in a duffel bag that had her initials on it, then found her blanket from when she was a newborn and tucked that away, too. She wondered what Jac was packing, but was still too annoyed to go and ask her. She was probably packing her sheet masks and dumb lip glosses or whatever. She was probably hoping to look good just in case they ran into Finn while fleeing their home.

By the time she was ready for bed, she was exhausted and fell asleep on top of the covers. It was still too hot for sheets and blankets, even though it was after ten at night, and Aggie dreamed of heat and shimmering skies and palm trees dancing against the moonlight, the sound of people laughing at a party, until the voices became louder and louder and then it just sounded like they were yelling, and her dad was trying to dance with her, shaking her by the shoulders.

"Aggie!" he kept saying, and when Aggie finally opened her eyes, she saw her dad standing over her, fear etched across his face, still wearing the same clothes that he had been wearing that night. He hadn't changed into his pajamas. "C'mon, kiddo," he said, pulling at her arm. "We gotta go."

"Where?" she said blearily, and then she heard the monotonous call of a voice over a loudspeaker.

". . . evacuations are now beginning for the Bird Streets neighborhoods!" she could hear, and suddenly Aggie was cold, way too cold.

"Did you pack your bag?" her dad asked. "Get it. Shoes are downstairs."

"Where's Jac?" Aggie asked as she sat up, trying to orient herself. Waking in the middle of the night always felt lonely and scary, but waking up like this was ten times worse. There were red lights flashing off her bedroom wall, and she heard the loudspeaker voice again. "Dad?"

"It's okay," he said. "Papa's getting Jac, and we're getting in the car, all right? Where's your bag?"

Aggie pointed at her half-zipped duffel bag, rubbing at her eyes, and her dad grabbed it and put it over his shoulder. And then he did something that he hadn't done in years: he grabbed Aggie and hoisted her up in his arms, carrying her out of the room.

Aggie felt like she should protest, but at the same time, she felt so afraid that she wasn't sure her legs would work and she'd be left behind. Instead, she clutched on to her dad's shirt as he ran down the stairs, calling out for her papa.

"On the way to the car!" he yelled back.

"Jac!" Aggie cried.

"I'm here!" Jac yelled, and Aggie felt herself go limp when she heard her sister's voice, all thoughts of their disastrous Halloween suddenly gone from her mind. She needed to see her sister, needed to get eyes on her so she knew that she wasn't just imagining Jac's voice, and when her dad went out the garage door, Aggie saw her papa also carrying Jac, who was in her pajamas and looking as bleary as Aggie felt.

As soon as Aggie's dad set her down inside the car, she grabbed Jac's hand and held on so, so tight.

Jac squeezed back just as hard.

The neighbors were running around as well, and Aggie watched as headlights after headlights lit up their dark street, the sounds of engines blazing to life echoing through the canyon. There were firetrucks at the end of their street, and the sky was orange like the most beautiful sunset.

It was the eeriest thing Aggie had ever seen.

"It's moving fast," Aggie's dad said, and her papa nodded, his mouth tight as he fastened his seat belt. "Did you get the hard drives with the baby photos?"

"And birth certificates and passports," he replied. "We're good. Let's go."

They were just pulling out of the driveway, when Aggie had a sudden, horrible thought. "Dads!" she cried. "Jack! Other Jack! Jack the Rat! We can't leave him behind. What if—"

"Aggs," Jac said, and just then a small black head and pink nose with long whiskers poked out of the top of Jac's pajama shirt. "I got him. Don't worry. His cage is in the trunk."

Aggie let out a sob and reached out to pet him. "Jack's family," she said, and her twin sister nodded next to her.

"Family doesn't get left behind," her dad agreed, and he turned left down the street and started to wind down the canyon with dozens of other cars. The smell of smoke was impossible to escape, and it felt like it was settling into Aggie's skin and hair like a fog or cloud, smothering her. She could see all the houses they had trick-or-treated at just a few hours earlier, and it almost seemed impossible that things could go from normal to frightening in such a short amount of time. Some houses still had dying, flickering jack-o'-lanterns on their front porches, the carved faces starting to sink in on themselves and become grotesque.

Aggie looked away and instead focused on the trail of red taillights in front of them, snaking their way down the road and into the distance. "Where are we going?" she asked in a small voice.

"Remember that hotel where we delivered the flowers?" her dad said, turning around in the passenger seat to face them. Aggie could tell he was trying to smile, but it didn't quite reach his eyes. "I called a friend who works there, and we're going there."

"Where is everyone else going, though?" Jac said. "What about our friends?"

"I'm sure everyone is on their way somewhere safe," her dad said from behind the wheel. "Just like we are."

Aggie tried to check her phone, but she didn't have any service, and next to her, she could see Jac doing the same thing. "Cell towers are down," she heard her dad mutter as he checked his own phone. And then he said a word that Aggie wasn't allowed to repeat.

She was so scared that she didn't even call him out on it.

There were more red lights flashing near the base of the canyon, shining off the "You Are Here" mirror at the Country Store that Aggie had taken her picture in only days before. What had seemed like a fun and positive message now seemed ominous and threatening, and Aggie shrank into her seat, squeezing Jac's hand again.

"Are you scared?" she whispered.

"Yes," Jac whispered back.

Horns honked ahead of them as their car inched

toward Sunset Boulevard, and Aggie saw the frightened faces of her neighbors in the cars around them. The sky was so bright that it felt like the afternoon, and helicopters swirled overhead, swooping down much lower than she had ever seen them before. It felt like something she'd watch on the internet or on the news, not something she'd ever experience in real life.

"We're going to be okay," her dad said again. "We're all together. We'll be okay."

Aggie had no choice but to believe him.

CHAPTER 14

JAC

The first things their dads did when they entered their hotel room was turn on the television to the local news while her papa immediately logged into the hotel Wi-Fi and flipped open his laptop.

The first thing Jac did was go into the bathroom, shut the door, turn on the shower, and throw up.

She hoped no one else could hear her. She didn't want to talk about it or explain how she felt. She was pretty sure it was mostly the smoke anyway, and she could still smell it all in her hair, coating her clothes. It felt like even her tongue had been dipped in ash, and in the mirror, she could see a streak of soot on her forehead. How could dust travel that fast and that far?

Jac waited to see if she was okay, then brushed her

teeth and climbed into the shower. The hot water would normally have felt unbearable under that terrible heat wave, but Jac turned it as hot as she could stand it, trying to rinse every last smoke molecule down the drain. She used the hotel's soap and shampoo and conditioner, annoyed with herself for not bringing her own toiletries from home. What had she packed anyway? Some pajamas and a few favorite books and her iPad? Seriously? That's what was important to her?! Her iPad?! What about that photo of her and Aggie when they were babies, posed in front of a jacaranda tree and next to a bushel of agapanthus? Or the birth ring her grandma had given them when she was five, the one that Jac kept in a special velvet box in the top drawer of her dresser. It didn't even fit her anymore, but she still loved it, still took it out to look at every now and then.

She had left those things behind, along with so many others, and Jac was terrified that she would never see them again.

Once she dried off and dug some fresh clothes out of her duffel bag, she got dressed and waited a beat before going back out into the hotel room. The hotel had put them in a mini suite, and Aggie was curled up next to her dad on the couch while their papa stood next to them, arms crossed and brow furrowed as they watched the fire blaze across the TV screen.

"Is that our neighborhood?" Jac whispered, and her dad reached out to her and pulled her down on the couch, tucking her under his other arm. It reminded Jac of birds folding their babies under their wings.

"It's the one right next to ours," her papa said, standing protectively over all three of them. He sounded oddly robotic, which is how he always acted whenever he got stressed out. Aggie and Jac called it "dad mode."

Their dad, on the other hand, had ordered french fries and mozzarella sticks.

At first Jac thought the food would just make her throw up again, but as she tentatively bit into a french fry, her nausea melted away. The salt and grease and potato felt like it soaked up the last tendrils of smoke that had swirled their way into her stomach, and from the corner of her eye, she saw Aggie reach for a mozzarella stick and chomp down.

It felt good to taste something when the rest of Jac felt so numb.

"You okay, kiddo?" her dad said, giving her a squeeze, and she nodded. "Did you hurl?"

She nodded again. "But I'm fine now," she said. "I feel better." She didn't point out that the rest of her family still smelled like smoke.

They nibbled and watched and sipped water for a while, all of them scared and stunned. It was impossible to think that anyone could stop that kind of inferno, but Jac could see firefighters on the screen, soaked in soot and sweat as they headed toward the fire. It was impossible to think that anyone's house could survive, and as the cameras panned across the hills, Jac could see the charred rubble of house after house, the fire dripping down the hills like slow-moving lava, swallowing everything in its path.

"Hey," their papa said as they sat around the coffee table eating, only Jac and her dad diving in while the others picked at the food. "We need to talk."

Aggie and Jac both nodded.

"I know there's a lot going on and your dad and I wanted to have this conversation tomorrow, but it's important." Their dads glanced at one another. "You two are sisters. We're your dads. We're a family, and we don't keep secrets from one another, okay? Not big ones, not like the ones you two have been keeping."

"Your papa and I love you so much," their dad said. "And we want to make sure that you know you can come to us, no matter what. And that no matter how you two go through life and experience it in different ways, that doesn't mean you can be cruel to one another."

"I know," Jac said.

"This is a bigger conversation," their dad said. "Probably one that we're going to have to have several times. But for now, I'm glad Papa and I are up to speed about what's going on with you two. We're here to support you. We've got your backs."

"Dad." Aggie had a tiny smile on her face. "Nobody actually says that anymore."

Jac knew that was Aggie was teasing him, mostly to lighten the mood a little, and she giggled before she could stop herself.

"Well, too bad, because that's what we've got," their dad replied while giving Aggie a loving nudge. "And we've got each other, no matter where we live or where we are, okay? It's the four of us, end of."

They hadn't done pinkie promises in a long time, but Jac held hers out now and thus began a lengthy and complicated series of pinkie promises exchanged over their lukewarm appetizers. "Deal," Aggie said, and when she and Jac linked fingers, Aggie squeezed extra tight.

Thank goodness Jac's phone buzzed just then, or otherwise she might have done something super embarrassing like starting to cry.

"It's Marnie!" she said, jumping up, and Aggie immediately followed her. "Can I answer?"

"Screen-time rules are out the window," her dad said, nodding at her, and Jac swiped on her phone to see Marnie's small face on the screen. She looked both angry and curious.

"Hi!" she said. "Oh my God, hiiiiiii. This is nuts, right? This is wild. Where are you?"

"At a hotel," Jac said, nibbling on another french fry. "We just left, like, an hour ago."

"I know, same," Marnie said, and then another familiar face squeezed into the screen.

"Dylan!" Aggie cried.

"Hi!" Dylan said. Her hair was tangled and rumpled like she had just been yanked out of bed, and Jac realized that she had probably looked the same pre-shower.

"Where are you?" she asked.

"We're at Dylan's dad's house," Marnie said. "He called her mom and told her to bring whoever needed a place to stay."

"What?" Aggie and Jac's dad hissed behind them. "They're at Dylan's dad's house?"

Jac waved at him to be quiet. That was the last thing they needed right then.

"That's so nice," she said instead. "Is, um, your mom also there, Dylan?"

"She sure is," Marnie answered for her, widening her eyes as if to say, *Save me.* "But so far everyone is behaving themselves and acting like grown-ups. Including my parents."

"Thank God," Dylan added from behind her, where she was chomping down on a fun-size Snickers bar.

"I'm stress eating," she said. "I already went through all the peanut M&M's."

"Yeah, we're watching the news," Aggie said, leaning over Jac's shoulder. "It's really scary."

"What about everyone else?" Jac said. "Tink and everybody?"

"Tink said that they're at her aunt's in Pacoima and that Josephine threw up twice in the car, so she's definitely not having a great night." Marnie started to tick the names off on her fingers while Dylan took the phone from her. "Taylor's family hasn't been evacuated yet, but they still left and went out to Taylor's grandma's house in Pasadena just to be safe. And Adriana's with her family at a hotel out in Thousand Oaks. I guess her mom has an account and points, so yeah, that's everyone."

"I'm surprised she didn't set up a lemonade stand at the base of the canyon," Dylan added, now breaking into a Kit Kat and handing half to Marnie.

"She definitely tried, I'll bet," Aggie said, and in the midst of a horrible night, it felt good to laugh about something silly and improper.

"At least we're all safe," Jac added, and out of the corner of her eye, she saw both her dads nod in tandem as they watched the screen.

"What'd you bring with you?" Dylan said. "I grabbed my homework and my teddy bear that I've had since I was born." She rolled her eyes at herself. "Real smart and useful, Dylan."

Marnie held up her Halloween pillowcase, still chock-full of candy. "I brought the important stuff," she said, then grinned. "My parents are so worked up that they're not even monitoring how much sugar I'm eating."

Jac laughed at that, imagining Marnie shoveling in as many candy bars as she could before her parents caught on.

"What's the news saying?" Dylan asked. "Our parents won't let us watch, and we're too scared to google it."

Jac flipped the screen so that they could see the TV. "Hey, maybe don't," her dad started to say, reaching for the phone. "If their parents don't want them . . ."

But then his voice trailed off, all of them falling silent as the camera zoomed out on the screen, revealing a steady stream of flames licking their way into their neighborhood.

"Oh no," Marnie said, not sounding nearly as tough as she normally did. "Oh no."

"Turn it off," Jac suddenly said. "I don't want to watch—turn it off!" She pushed her phone into Aggie's hands, her fingers trembling so hard she was afraid she'd drop it and shatter the screen. When her dads couldn't find the remote fast enough, Jac turned on her heel and went blindly down the hall and into the bedroom, stumbling until she found the light switch. Nothing was familiar, not the carpet or the smell of detergent or the bedspread that felt slippery under her hands as she sank down onto the bed. Everything Jac wanted was suddenly miles away, about to be burned up and turned to ash and spread to the wind, and she put her hands over her face, embarrassed to be crying.

Her papa found her a minute later, sinking down next to her on the bed and wrapping her up in his arms. Even under the smoke and sweat, he still smelled like himself, like home, and Jac clung to him, scared of what would happen if he let go.

"I know, bug," he whispered. "Me too."

She fell asleep on the slippery bed sometime around four a.m., and when she woke up a few hours later, Aggie was curled up next to her, her feet tucked under Jac's legs. Jac could see dried tears on her sister's face as well, and she sat up a little to see her dad asleep on the queen bed next to theirs. She could hear their papa talking on the phone down the hall, voice low and serious in between long pauses, and Jac was pretty sure she could smell coffee, too.

"Jac," her dad whispered. "Go back to sleep."

"Is our house okay?" she whispered back.

"Not sure yet," he said. "But it's just stuff, bug. We have what matters."

For some reason, that made Jac feel better even though it should have made her feel worse. She reached down and pulled the sheet up over her and Aggie, and her sister snuggled closer to her in her sleep. The air-conditioning was cold in a good way, making Jac want to get warmer, and she tucked herself next to Aggie and closed her eyes again.

When she woke up next, Aggie was kneeling next to her, holding out a blueberry muffin. "I saved this for you," she said.

Jac blinked a few times, feeling sticky and tired and disoriented. "What time is it?" she mumbled.

"Almost ten," Aggie said.

Jac sat up a little. It was sunny out, but the air was still heavy with smoke, making the whole world look darkly pink and weirdly apocalyptic. "Is our house okay?" she asked, taking the muffin.

"I don't know," Aggie said, sitting down next to her and leaning back against the headboard. "We can't tell from TV or the news. Dads said that the fire crew managed to stop the fire from taking over the whole neighborhood, but it still got some houses."

Jac started to pick out the blueberries with her fingernails, eating them one at a time. She hadn't really had dinner the night before, and had thrown up most of it anyway, and she was surprised to find that she was starving. "Can we get omelets?" she asked. "I could eat a horse."

"Gross," Aggie said, but she was already hopping down off the bed. "Dads!" she called. "Good news! Jac's awake and she's hungry!"

By the time they had eaten and showered and gotten dressed in the clothes that they had hastily grabbed, all four of them were restless. Jac suspected that their dads had ingested way too much caffeine, judging from the way they were texting and calling and pacing back and forth across the room. Jac was just about to suggest, only half-jokingly, that they go down to the hotel gym and burn off some of that energy when her phone buzzed again, this time Marnie's face filled the screen, looking wide-eyed and stricken.

"Hi," she said breathlessly. "So. I have news. Dylan's parents got into the neighborhood."

And suddenly Jac's dads were grabbing the phone away from her. "Hey!" she protested. "Marnie's *my* friend!"

"My friend, too!" Aggie said.

They just ignored her.

"Oh hi, Mr. and Mr. Palmer," Marnie said, suddenly sounding *very* polite and formal.

"Did Dylan's parents see the houses?" their dad asked.

"How did they even get into the neighborhood?"

Marnie paused. "Well, they're *famous*," she said, like that explained everything. "Adriana always says that's the one true currency in Los Angeles."

Jac's papa closed his eyes very briefly and took a deep breath before asking, "Did they say what they saw?"

"Oh yeah." Marnie's voice went serious again, and for the first time since they had left their trick-or-treating excursion, Jac wondered why Tink wasn't running everything the way she normally did, why Dylan and Marnie were the ones who kept calling them.

And then her stomach started to sink.

"So, it seems like everyone else's house is okay," Marnie started to say, "but Tink's grandma's house . . ." She trailed off.

"Oh my God," her dad said.

"It was really old and had wood shingles and was the last house on the street," Marnie said. "That's what my mom said. And it's right on the edge of the canyon and . . ." She trailed off again. "It's gone."

"All of it?" Aggie asked, her voice high and squeaky.

"I think so," Marnie said. "That's what my dad said. He's going out to talk to them now, he and my mom together. Tink's mom and my mom were in birthing classes together; they've known each other for years." Her eyes filled with tears as she added, "I just feel so bad."

Jac reached for the phone again, and this time, her papa handed it back to her. Jac hated how she felt inside, so grateful and relieved that her house was still standing and so sick and sad that Tink's house wasn't there anymore. Judging from the look on Marnie's face, she felt the same way.

"When can we all go home?" Jac asked her as both her dads reached for their own phones.

"I'm not sure," Marnie said. "I hope soon? I wish we could all be together again. I can't believe Halloween was just last night. It feels like it was a million years ago."

Aggie squeezed into the frame next to Jac, and for the first time in a long while, Jac was grateful for her sister's closeness, not irritated by it. "Me too," Aggie said. "This has been the worst twenty-four hours ever."

"It'll be over soon," Jac said, trying to sound reassuring and not entirely succeeding. "We'll all be back home soon."

"But Tink . . ." Aggie said, and all three girls fell silent, looking at each other through the tiny screen.

"Hey," Marnie said. "We're a team, right? Tink more than anyone."

"Yep," Jac said, popping the *p* at the end of the word. "We'll get through it."

Privately, though, she wasn't quite sure.

It took two days before they could all go home again, and nobody was happier about it than Jac and Aggie. Two days stuck in a hotel room (even if it was a very nice, fancy hotel room) with their dads was way too much togetherness.

Still, Jac found herself holding her breath as their car climbed up the hill to their house. Both sides of the street were smoldering as they got up to their neighborhood, trees and brush and wildflowers all gone. The Country Store was open, and Lilly's Coffee Cart was there, too, with a huge line of people outside. Jac wasn't sure if they needed caffeine or they just wanted to be supportive, but either way, it made her happy to see it.

The air wasn't exactly clear, but beyond the smoke, the skies were blue again, and as they went up their windy road toward home, there were police officers and firemen (firepeople? Jac wondered, and decided she would have to google that once she had internet service again) lining the street, waving the people up and checking IDs and drivers' licenses. "Go ahead," the police officer said to them once he confirmed that the address on Jac's dad's license matched the location where they were heading, and Jac held her breath as they drove up their street, every house standing. But just two blocks over, she could see the gaping holes of the houses that had been there, the charred land and still-smoking piles of ash, brick chimneys demolished into rubble.

It looked like a movie, not like real life.

But then they were at their house, and it was still standing and sturdy, and even though Jac had been there for less than three months, even though she had thought that this new place would never feel like home, she had never been so happy to see a building in her life.

"We're back!" Aggie screamed as they ran inside, and Jac could smell smoke and see soot stains on the wall, but she could also see the sunlight coming in through their kitchen, and their old sofa that one dad hated and the other adored, and she could see up the stairs into Aggie's bedroom, and after so much uncertainty and change and fear, Jac grinned and impulsively hugged the banister.

And then she thought about Tink and Josephine and their family and felt bad all over again.

"Home!" Aggie cried, spinning in a circle around their living room. "I never want to stay in a hotel again!"

In fact, the only living thing that had had a *fantastic* time in the hotel was Jack the Rat, who had feasted on room service (they had forgotten to grab his kibble for him), peed in the bathtub, slept nestled between his two favorite people (obviously Jac and Aggie, Jack the Rat had zero use for their dads), and had napped in the sunshine while overlooking the pool and cabanas. Jack the Rat was sorry to come back home and wondered when they would get to go on vacation again.

Word spread quickly that the twins were back home with their dads, and pretty soon all their phones started to buzz. "You should just come over," their dad finally said.

"Yeah," Jac said into her own phone, talking to Adriana. Their internet was still down, so they could only call, not text. "It's like being a pioneer," Jac had said, and both of her dads had immediately groaned and buried their faces in their hands.

"You should just come over," she told her, echoing her dad.

And within an hour, it felt like the whole neighborhood was streaming down the street and into their house.

Adriana and her older sister Gabriella and their parents showed up first, carrying two giant jugs of—what else?—lemonade. "It's on the house," Adriana said, and then hugged both girls for a very long time. Across the room, their dads had put an old record on their turntable since they couldn't stream any music, and then they came rushing over to introduce themselves to Adriana's parents and take the lemonade from them. "Come in, please. We don't really have much food but we do have some sparkling water," Jac's papa said. "Honey, where's the SodaStream?"

Taylor's family showed up next, looking a little bedraggled but otherwise okay, and carrying a platter of sandwiches and several bags of chips. "The Country Store wouldn't let us pay for any of it," Taylor said. "Isn't that so nice?" Then she paused and added, "Can I see your rat?"

"Their what?" her mom said before Jac's dad quickly ushered Taylor's parents into the living room.

Marnie and her little brother and her mom showed up with a bunch of two-liter bottles of soda, which all the kids quickly attacked before the adults could stop them, and then Dylan and her parents came to the front door. Her mom was holding what looked like a fruit-and-cheese tray from somewhere very fancy, and her dad was holding a bottle of dark liquid that Jac was pretty sure was off-limits for the kids. Dylan seemed both nervous and pleased to be there, and both Aggie and Jac gave their parents a stern look before letting Dylan's family into the foyer.

Luckily, their dads were on their best behavior and welcomed everyone inside before ushering them through the kitchen and onto the patio. Most of the parents were outside chatting, sharing stories of emergency evacuation, nightmare conversations with insurance agencies, lucky breaks that allowed their houses to still be standing.

Jac and Aggie, being excellent hosts, grabbed a

bag of Cool Ranch Doritos, a bottle of Sprite, a stack of paper cups, and whisked their friends upstairs and away from all the boring conversation.

Everyone poked around their bedrooms for a while, commenting on Aggie's stack of Magic Tree House books and Jac's neatly organized collection of lip glosses. They finally settled around Jac's bed, the trundle pulled out so that they could accommodate everyone.

"Someone's missing," Adriana said, pushing her glasses up on her nose.

"*Two* people are missing," Jac said, thinking of Josephine twirling around them on Halloween night. "I tried calling Tink, but she didn't answer."

"I texted her," Adriana said. "We had reception at the hotel before we left. I just told her that everyone was coming here. She didn't respond, but I know she saw it."

"That must be so weird to have a house and then not have one," Marnie said with a sigh. "It's not even like you moved or anything. It's just gone."

"Do you think they'll have to move?" Aggie asked, sounding sad.

"Maybe?" Dylan said. "I guess they could build their house again, but maybe they don't want to. Maybe they don't even want to come back here anymore."

Jac was about to say something to that when she

heard a car pull up in the driveway, and immediately, all six girls ran to the window and looked out. Tink's mom's car was parking behind a stack of cars, and they all watched as Tink and Josephine climbed out of the back seat and Tink's mom hurried around to the passenger seat to help their grandma out of the car.

Jac had never seen Tink and Josephine look so serious before.

She started to head downstairs to tell everyone that Tink and her family were there, but before she could even leave the room, they were already outside, greeting them and helping Tink's grandma and welcoming them inside for snacks and drinks. "Everyone's brought enough food for the entire neighborhood," she heard her dad say, and then he gave Tink's mom a hug, one that she desperately seemed to need.

All the girls tumbled downstairs, making it sound like a team of horses were colliding into each other, and as soon as the front door open, they all froze, suddenly and collectively unsure of what to do. Did they hug Tink? Say they were sorry? Offer to babysit Josephine?

Jac realized that the next move was up to her. "C'mon," she said. "We have chips and soda upstairs. Josephine, you can come, too."

"No, thank you," Josephine whispered, clinging

to her mom's hand, and even Tink looked unsure, but her mom smiled at her even as she wrapped an arm around Josephine's shoulders.

"Go ahead, honey," her mom said. "We'll be downstairs if you need us."

"Come on," Adriana said, and then she was pulling Tink away from her family and the girls swallowed her up into the center of their herd as they went back upstairs, Jac shutting the door behind them for good measure.

Not sure what to do, she got Tink a cup of chips and another cup of soda. "We have more things downstairs if you want," she said. "And a bunch of Halloween candy, too."

Instead, Tink sat down on Jac's bed and started to cry.

Aggie was the first to move, scooting up next to her friend and putting her arms around her. Marnie followed next, followed by Taylor and Dylan and Adriana, and then Jac set down the snacks and joined them.

None of them said a word because there was nothing to say. Downstairs, a sad-sounding woman was singing about songbirds and knowing the score, and Jac hoped that it wasn't too upsetting for Tink. Her dads must have had the same thought because the song suddenly changed to something a lot livelier.

Tink cried and cried until Jac finally went to get a box of tissues for her, and then Dylan coached her through some deep breaths and Taylor rubbed her back. "It just sucks," she finally said, wiping her eyes. "It was my grandma's house. She'd lived there for fifty years! And now we don't have anywhere to go except my aunt's house out in dumb Pacoima and I'll have to change schools and . . . what happens to our team?"

"Hey," Jac said, playfully serious. "Nobody breaks up our team."

Tink gave her a watery, wobbly smile. "I'm sorry I was such a brat about your Halloween costume," she sniffled.

"I'm sorry I didn't realize how important it was to you," Jac replied.

"And you're absolutely not moving!" Adriana said. "We'll figure it out!"

"Actually," Taylor said quietly, and all heads swiveled to look at her. "My mom and dad were going to talk to your mom and grandma about it tonight, but we were going to see if you and your family wanted to come live with us for a while."

Tink's eyes looked like they were about to fall out of their head, they were so big.

"We have that guesthouse in the back that nobody uses," Taylor said quickly, mistaking Tink's shock for horror. "And if that's not big enough, you and Josephine could just come stay in the house with us and your mom and grandma and Finn could stay in the guest-house. And it wouldn't be forever, you know, but that way you could stay in school and we could all stay together and you'd still be in the neighborhood. Right?" Taylor bit her lip.

Tink started to cry again. "That's so nice!" she sobbed.

"Well, you and your family were so nice to us!" Taylor said, and now her eyes were wet, too. "When I was going through everything and some people weren't nice . . ." She swallowed hard. "You and your mom and grandma, all of you were really kind."

Tink wiped her nose on the back of her wrist, and Aggie quickly passed her another tissue before she could get snot on Jac's bedsheets. "Do you have any water, maybe?" Tink asked.

Jac leapt to her feet, glad to be useful. "Be right back," she said, then hurried out of the room and down the stairs. She found the jug of filtered water in the refrigerator and added some ice to it. She never thought she'd find the sound of the refrigerator hum so soothing, but it was. It sounded normal. It sounded like home.

Out on the patio, she could see that Taylor's parents had pulled Tink's mom and grandma aside and were speaking to them quietly. Tink's mom's eyes were wet, and Jac felt a tiny surge of relief that at least some things would stay the same, even if so much had changed.

And that's when she realized that Josephine was missing.

A quick scan of the patio didn't reveal the seven-year-old among the adults, and Jac did a fast tour of the downstairs, peeking behind doors and in bathrooms. She could only imagine what Josephine could get up to by herself, and just as Jac went outside to alert their dads to a missing kid, she saw a small pink sneaker dangling off the porch from around the corner.

Jac wound her way around the adults and went over to the side of the house, slipping around the corner where she found a very sad-looking Josephine sitting by herself, holding what looked like a brand-new stuffed koala. She didn't even look up when Jac sat down next to her.

"Hey," Jac said. "Did you get bored with all the grown-ups?"

Josephine shrugged, still looking at the ground.

"Do you want to come upstairs with us? Tink's there."

"No, thank you," Josephine said, sounding very small.

Jac nodded to herself and rubbed her hands on her thighs, trying to figure out what to do. "Do you want to do some cartwheels?" she said. "We can go out in the front yard. There's a whole bunch of space out there; you can do as many as you want."

"No, thank you," Josephine said again.

This was bad. In the weeks before, during practice, Jac would have happily shot Josephine with a tranquilizer just to get her to calm down a bit, but seeing her like this was both depressing and unsettling.

Finally, Jac had a thought. "Do you want to tell me some fun facts about penguins?"

At first it seemed like that idea was a failure as well, and she was about to leave Josephine and go upstairs to get Tink when Josephine said, "Okay."

"Great!" Jac said, probably too loudly, but Josephine didn't seem to mind.

"The Emperor penguin is the largest species of penguins," she said quietly.

"Wow, that's awesome."

"And? And the smallest one is the fairy penguin. It's really cute. It looks like a baby seal kinda. And the chinstrap penguin takes ten thousand naps a day." Josephine took a deep breath and, for the first time that day, started to sound like her normal self, and Jac put an arm around her shoulders and settled in, very happy to learn all that Josephine could tell her, very relieved that they were back home, and very grateful that everyone was or would soon be where they belonged.

CHAPTER 15

AGGIE

After the sun set and Jac brought Josephine back to her mom and the girls upstairs demolished all the chips and soda, they came back downstairs just as Marnie's dad was walking into the house with a bunch of pizzas. Marnie ran to him, hugging him around the waist, which he returned while also trying to not drop ten different pies. Aggie helpfully took some of the boxes from him, secretly hoping that there'd be a plain cheese pizza in there somewhere.

They all sat around the kitchen after that, digging into various boxes and pouring water and sodas for everyone. "We need to do something," Adriana said. "This is bad for our whole neighborhood, and *I'm* a local business owner. *I* should do something."

"We could sell brownies," Dylan offered.

"In this town?" Adriana gave her a "duh" look. "No way. And it has to be something bigger."

"What if we do like a fundraiser?" Aggie said, eating her second slice of plain cheese. "Like a talent show."

Tink's eyes were starting to get bigger and bigger, and she flung her own slice of pepperoni down onto her plate. "What about a baseball game?" she said. "Kids versus parents!"

"Yes!" Adriana said. "We could sell tickets and then donate the money."

"I liked the talent show idea," Josephine said, and Aggie had zero doubt she had been picturing herself cartwheeling across the stage. She wasn't sure what had happened earlier, but Jac had disappeared downstairs to get water and returned with Josephine in tow, who had immediately curled up next to Tink.

"We could play at Laurel Canyon Park," Tink continued, and now she was scrambling to her feet, pizza forgotten. "And sell tickets, like Adriana said, and maybe we can advertise—"

"I can do that," Dylan's mom said, and then looked shy when every head swiveled in her direction. "I mean, I have a strong following on social media. Might as well do some good with it, right?"

Dylan beamed as she hugged her mom.

They all started to talk and plan, and then Aggie ran upstairs to get her iPad so they could take notes.

Most of the parents were all for it, and Adriana's dad offered to sit out the game so that Adri could play and he'd man the lemonade stand instead.

"Brave man," Jac muttered in Aggie's ear, and she giggled.

It took two weeks of planning and phone calls, a few living room meetings, and a Zoom with a bunch of capital-H Housewives, but there was a huge buzz of excitement in the neighborhood. Dylan's mom had even started a GoFundMe for Tink's family, which generated so much money that they were able to expand it to more families who had lost their homes, and Aggie and her dad spent thirty minutes one night refreshing the page, watching the amount grow.

"You know how Dad and I always say that you and Jac are going to college?" Aggie's dad said.

"Yeah?" Aggie said.

"I changed my mind. I want you two to be reality-TV stars instead."

Aggie had laughed for a long, long time after that.

By the time the Saturday before Thanksgiving rolled around, Aggie woke up early. Their house still had a faint whiff of smoke to it, especially in the early mornings as the city started to wake up, and it gave her a small spark of anxiety. But before she could do anything about it, Jac burst into her room, wrinkled pj's and bedhead everywhere.

"Today's the day!" she screamed, tackling Aggie

back into bed. "We're going to crush it!"

And just like that, the anxiety was gone.

They had a busy morning of packing snacks and (to their parents' irritation) letting Jack the Rat run around the house for a bit. "He has lots of nervous energy," Aggie said. "He has to burn it off."

"He has an entire *wheel* in his cage," their dad pointed out, quickly moving their shoes away from the front door before Jack the Rat could set his sights on them. "Could have gotten a fish, but nope." He sighed.

There was also a flurry of FaceTime calls that morning. Their dads had temporarily suspended their weekend phone bans just so the girls could stay in contact with their friends, and both Aggie and Jac took full advantage of it. "Are you FaceTiming and eating cereal at the same time?" their dad asked Aggie at one point, who looked befuddled at the question.

"Of course!"

"Hi, Mr. Palmer!" Marnie yelled from the screen. "See you today! We're going to *crush* you!"

"Thanks, Marnie," their dad said, then gave Aggie a quick kiss to the top of her head before going upstairs.

By the time the game rolled around, Aggie and Jac were practically vibrating with energy and tumbled out of the car toward their friends. Already the bleachers were crowded, and they saw some of their neighbors and kids from school, and even more people who they didn't even recognize. "Wow," Aggie said. "Everyone really showed up."

"Hiiiiii!" Josephine screamed, running toward them. Aggie put her hands out to catch her before she could attack them with a hug. Josephine was small, but she moved fast. "We made so much money!"

"Josephine!" Tink called. "We need both of them. Let's not wrestle them to the ground quite yet!" But she looked happier than she had in a long time, her smile wide and her cheeks flushed, and she hugged both girls tight when she was close enough. She and Taylor had been sharing a room at Taylor's house, with Finn and Josephine staying in the guesthouse with their mom and grandma. "We are peas in a pod" was how Josephine described it, and while it sounded like a tight fit, Aggie knew they were grateful for the space.

"At least it's not Pacoima" was how Tink described the situation.

They left their dads back with the adults while they went over to their friends on the bench near the dugout. They had tried to coordinate outfits, but with eight of them of various shapes and sizes and tastes, it was tricky. Finally Taylor had just said, "They'll know we're on the same team. We're the only kids out there," and they all had to admit she had a point.

"Where's Adriana?" Jac asked. "She's never late."

“Oh, she’s not late,” Dylan said with a laugh, pointing across the dugout to where Adriana had set up her lemonade stand and was advising her dad, binder in hand.

“Can you please go get her?” Tink said. “We need to warm up, and she’s been explaining the stand to her dad for the last twenty minutes. What’s there to explain? It’s lemonade. You pour it.”

“Don’t let her hear you say that.” Taylor laughed and headed toward the pitcher’s mound to start practicing.

After several quick games of rock-paper-scissors, Aggie lost and was elected to go get Adriana. “Adri!” she yelled. “C’mon, we have to start getting ready.”

“Hold on, I’m just explaining the cash box!” she said. “Okay, Dad, this is serious. No bills over twenty dollars, okay?”

“You do realize I’m an engineer who can add, right?” her dad said, but he looked more amused than anything.

“That binder looks huge!” Aggie added.

“Thirty-two pages!” Adriana’s dad said, shaking it a little. “Including three on what to do in case of a tsunami.”

“Run,” Aggie said. “That’s what we should do. You don’t need three pages for that.”

Adriana pointedly ignored them both. “And don’t

forget that anyone who bought a ticket to the event gets ten percent off their purchase, and twenty percent off if they purchase our new lemonade-cherry slushie. But no more than that! We're raising money for charity here!"

"I'm both very proud and very scared of you," her dad replied, and Adriana smiled at that.

Aggie finally managed to drag her friend away from the stand and waved to her dads, who were doing some form of stretching that made them look not limber at all. Dylan's mom was chatting with them, and Aggie hoped they weren't embarrassing their family.

By the time the game was about to start, the stands were full and people lined the field, sitting on blankets and under sun umbrellas, cheering and yelling encouragement to both teams. The girls graciously allowed their parents to bat first. ("*Strategy*," Tink said, nodding like she knew state secrets.)

Just before they took to the field, Taylor started to frown at something in the distance. "Wait," she said, and Aggie followed her gaze to see a crowd of boys running toward the field, all of them wearing matching shirts. As soon as they got to the fence, they stood in a line, cheering loudly, and Taylor let out a soft gasp. "That's my old baseball team," she said.

All of the boys' shirts said "TEAM TAYLOR" in bright letters.

"Let's go, Taylor!" one of the boys yelled.

"Pitch a shutout!" another one called.

Aggie felt her eyes get wet as a huge smile spread across Taylor's face, and across the field, she could see both of Taylor's parents wiping away tears.

Tink was grinning, too, and she gave Taylor a hug. "Let's do this," she said, and Taylor nodded as she jogged out to the pitcher's mound.

For old people, their parents were *good* players. Dylan's mom never even dropped a single ball behind home plate, Taylor's dad threw excellent curve balls, and even Aggie and Jac's dads fielded like . . . well, not like pros, but better than Aggie and Jac thought they could do. Marnie's parents even pulled off a double play, and Marnie cheered wildly at that. "Teamwork makes the dream work!" she yelled as her parents gave each other a high five.

At one point, Adriana had to step out and go help her dad with the lemonade stand, where there was a crowd. "One line!" she cried as she ran over. "Nice and orderly! There's enough for everyone!" Aggie hoped that there would be enough lemonade-cherry slushies left over after the game because they looked really good.

By the bottom of the ninth inning, the score was 4–3, with the girls' team barely clinging to the lead. Aggie had hit a homer with Tink and Marnie on base and then Dylan managed to steal not one but *two* bases, cackling wildly to herself as she crossed home plate. But then Tink's mom hit a grounder that got away from Jac, and she, Adriana's mom, and Marnie's dad ran like mad around the bases. Tink's grandmother had cheered from the sidelines, waving two pom-poms. "That's my girl!" she had yelled.

Taylor did her thing and struck out two of the parents, but then Jac and Aggie's dad managed to hit a single, and Jac pretended not to know him when he arrived at first base. "Your dad just did that," he said, looking flushed and proud of himself.

Parents. They were so cute sometimes.

Finally, Dylan's mom stepped up to the plate, swinging a few times and then smiling in the direction of her assistant, who was no doubt taking pictures for her social media feeds. (She and Dylan had struck a deal: Nothing posted until the day after the event.) "Let's go, Taylor!" Aggie yelled. "Let's strike her out and wrap this up!"

Taylor's first pitch was a strike, but then her second sailed smoothly over the plate and Dylan's mom sent it flying.

Right toward left field.

"Oh no," said every single girl on the field.

"Josephine!" Tink shrieked. "Heads up!"

Josephine, who had been admiring a tiny yellow

buttercup in the field, looked up and gasped.

The ball seemed to move in slow motion as it soared through the air, arcing down toward their youngest player, and Aggie sighed to herself. Well, it had been a fun game, and they had made a lot of money for their neighborhood. That's what mattered.

The ball came closer and closer to Josephine, and she swallowed hard, stuck her glove up in the air. . . .

And caught it.

"Oh my God!" Tink screamed.

"What?!" Aggie cried.

"Did I win?" Josephine asked.

They all ran toward to her, yelling and cheering, and Josephine grinned as they grabbed her up in a group hug. "We won!" Jac cried. "Josephine won the game!"

"I did?" Josephine said.

Even the parents were cheering for them, and Tink's mom also came running over to hug her youngest kid. "So proud of you!" she said. "My baby!"

"Can we get lemonades now?" Josephine asked. "I'm hot."

"Lemonades for everyone!" Adriana said. "Thirty percent off!"

Aggie caught Jac's eye and they both grinned, and this time Aggie felt like she was finally home.

CHAPTER 16

JAC

"I'm sunburned," Jac said as she sat down next to Aggie on their back porch. The sun was just starting to disappear behind the skyline, making the sky a beautiful swirl of yellows and pinks. "I think I need to do a sheet mask tonight." Then she hesitated before adding, "You could use one of mine. You know, if you want."

"No thanks," Aggie said, sipping from her soda. "They make you look like a serial killer." But then she grinned at Jac. Her glove was still in her lap, a dusty relic from the game.

"They do," Jac agreed. Ever since the end of the game, there had been a peace between her and Aggie that hadn't been there in a long, long time. Maybe

Marnie had been right: Teamwork *did* make the dream work.

"I, uh," Aggie started to say, fidgeting with her glove. "I'm sorry I've been such a jerk to you, especially with all the birthday stuff, Finn stuff, and everything."

"Me too," Jac said quietly. She had the weird feeling that if she looked at Aggie, she would start to cry, so she kept her eyes focused on the ground.

"I just get worried sometimes that when you do different things than me, it's that you don't like me."

"What?" Jac's head shot up. "Aggie, that's so stupid! Why wouldn't I like you?"

"Because, I don't know, sometimes it feels like you're growing up and growing away."

"Just because I want to eat sushi doesn't mean I don't like you," Jac said. "What would I do without my twin sister? Who would help me raise our dads?"

Aggie laughed at that. "Remember when Dad tried to use the paper map and we got lost? Or when Papa couldn't change the ringtone on his phone?"

"They'd be so doomed without us," Jac agreed. "And I'm sorry, too. I never wanted to make you feel like I didn't like you or want to be like you. I just . . . I don't know, I just want to do things differently than you sometimes."

"I know," Aggie said. "That's okay. I know you'll

always be my sister." Then she paused before adding, "I'm still going to Cheesecake Factory, though."

Jac smiled. "Well, I still think you'll like crispy rice."

"That's what Dad said, but I have my doubts," Aggie replied.

"Guess we'll find out," Jac said, then scooted closer to her sister and rested her head on her shoulder. "I love you, Agapanthus," she said. "There's no one else I'd rather be twins with than you."

"Well, good thing, because we really look a lot alike," Aggie said, but then she took her sister's hand and squeezed. "Love you, too, Jacaranda."

They sat in silence for a few minutes, enjoying the peace and quiet, before they heard a scream from inside the house.

"WHERE IS JACK THE RAT?" their dad yelled. "NOT A DRILL! THE RAT IS LOOSE!"

Aggie and Jac grinned at one another; then Aggie tugged on her glove and stood up.

"Play ball," Jac said, and they hurried toward their dads and into their home.

ACKNOWLEDGMENTS

Thank you to Lisa Grubka at United Talent Agency for championing and supporting this book when it was just a few sentences in my brain, and I had no idea how it would end. (Spoiler alert: I figured it out eventually.)

A very big dose of gratitude to Emilia Rhodes, Kristen Pettit, and Alyson Day for kindly shepherding this book through all of its various stages, and to the team at HarperCollins, including Karina Williams, Kristen Eckhardt, Jessica Berg, Mark Rifkin, and Jacqueline Hornberger.

Thank you to the librarians, teachers, educators, parents, and guardians who work to make sure all kinds of kids have access to all kinds of books, and for supporting my books throughout the years.

Thank you to all of the parents who spoke with me so candidly and honestly about what it's like raising kids in the twenty-first century, especially in Los

Angeles. Your children are so fortunate to have you guiding them through this messy, wonderful world.

Thank you to Anna for being this book's very first reader and for catching my typos. Thank you to Stella for all of the fun penguin facts, and for letting me know what happens at piano recitals these days. Thank you to Lena for spending a Sunday morning telling me all about middle school. You are all amazing and your moms are pretty awesome, too.

Thank you to the real-life Adriana for letting me use both her name and her love of spreadsheets, and for being such an incredible friend for so many years.

My immense gratitude to Pascal Campion and Julia Feingold for creating the most beautiful cover and for capturing that magic hour sunset light that always reminds me why I choose to live in Southern California.

And as always and forever, thank you to my brilliant family, especially my two favorite people. I love you more than Josephine loves penguins.